THE GOODBYE GIRLS

ADVANCE PRAISE FOR THE GOODBYE GIRLS

"Funny the mess people can make of their love lives—or at least it is in *The Goodbye Girls*, Lisa Harrington's hilarious deep dive into the chaos of high school romance and revenge."
–**Vicki Grant**, award-winning author of *36 Questions that Changed My Mind About You*

"Lisa Harrington is the Queen of Dialogue. Her words pull you into the teenage world with an effortless, snappy sense of humour, and realistic portrayal of the ups and downs of friendships and family. She makes writing look easy."
–**Daphne Greer**, Silver Birch–shortlisted author of *Jacob's Landing*

"Lisa Harrington's teen dialogue is always spot on and doesn't disappoint in her latest offering. Paired with a fast-paced plot that expertly weaves in deeper layers of family secrets and best-friend drama, *The Goodbye Girls* holds you in its grip until the end."
–**Jo Ann Yhard**, author of *Lost on Brier Island*

THE GOODBYE GIRLS

LISA HARRINGTON

NIMBUS
PUBLISHING
— NIMBUS.CA —

Nimbus Publishing Limited
3660 Strawberry Hill St, Halifax, NS, B3K 5A9
(902) 455-4286 nimbus.ca

Printed and bound in Canada
Cover design: Cyanotype Book Architects
Interior design: Grace Laemmler Design
NB1292

This novel is a work of fiction. Names, characters, incidents, and places, including organizations and institutions, either are the product of the author's imagination or are used fictitiously.

Library and Archives Canada Cataloguing in Publication
Harrington, Lisa, Author
The goodbye girls / Lisa Harrington.
Issued in print and electronic formats.
ISBN 978-1-77108-635-6 (softcover).
ISBN 978-1-77108-636-3 (HTML)
I. Title.
PS8615.A7473G66 2018   jC813'.6   C2017-907932-8
                                       C2017-907933-6

Canada

Nimbus Publishing acknowledges the financial support for its publishing activities from the Government of Canada through the Canada Book Fund (CBF) and the Canada Council for the Arts, and from the Province of Nova Scotia. We are pleased to work in partnership with the Province of Nova Scotia to develop and promote our creative industries for the benefit of all Nova Scotians.

CHAPTER 1

AN EAR-PIERCING SHRIEK RINGS OUT ACROSS THE high school cafeteria. The kind that makes your eyes automatically squeeze shut and your insides scrunch up. When it ends, I stretch my neck to see above the crowd. I've heard that shriek before. I live with it—Trish.

I don't know how I see it from so far away; I just do. A splotch of red against pink. It glows like it's on fire.

"Here. Hold this." I shove my lunch tray at Willa.

"Hey, just a sec!" she exclaims, struggling to balance my tray on top of hers. "It's not like I can just grow an extra arm out of my butt!"

I stomp over to Trish's table practically frothing at the mouth. She doesn't see me coming. "Is that…" I place both my hands flat on the end of her table, "*ketchup* on my brand new T-shirt?" I say it real quiet, letting the words leak out through my teeth.

Her eyes widen when she sees me standing there. "Uh… hey, Lizzie." She quickly reaches for some napkins and starts blotting the red spot, rubbing it in to the soft pink fabric, making it worse.

"I repeat. Is that ketchup on my brand new T-shirt?"

"Um…."

It's as if I can hear her frantically shuffling the words around inside her head, arranging them into some kind of order that will make sense.

Finally her head snaps up. "You know, Lizzie, you could show a little more concern, like, for my well-being."

"*What?*"

"Well, what if this is blood or something? Like maybe I got injured. Did you ever think of that?"

I straighten up and fold my arms. "If you did, you probably deserved it."

Olivia, one of Trish's friends, gasps dramatically and slaps her hand to her chest. "You shouldn't say stuff like that!"

"Yeah, Lizzie. Real nice," Trish says all snarky.

Like all this is my *fault.* "Gimme my shirt back." I hold out my hand. "You didn't even ask if you could borrow it."

"Oh. What. I'm just supposed to strip off, right here and now?"

I shrug. "Whatever it takes."

From behind me a voice says, "It was an accident, Lizzie."

My breath forms a little hiccup in my throat. I turn. It's Garret.

"Todd and I were messin' around," he says. "He frisbeed his tray across the table and it flipped one of those ketchup cups right onto Trish's…."

There are numerous snickers from around the table.

"Boob!" someone shouts.

Garret's cheeks redden. "Uh...*chest* area."

Garret MacLeod. If Disney's Prince Charming could take a human form, it would be Garret MacLeod. A senior, co-president of student government, on the football team, awesome drummer, with a smile that turns my legs into silly putty. He only has one fault—he's been going out with my sister, Trish, for almost four months.

I lean in close to Trish and whisper, "You're a dead woman." Then I make my way back to my part of the cafeteria, the part designated for the "tenners"—the unworthy, invisible grade tens.

"Your potato wedges are cold," Willa says, sliding me my tray. "They're probably gonna be sort of gross."

"Story of my life," I grumble.

"I saw you talking to Garret. So things can't be *that* bad." She glances back over at Trish's table. "Do you think he was born that way? Or is it something he practices?"

"It can't be learned," I say, like I'm an expert. "You either got it, or you don't."

Willa sighs. "I've been in love with that guy since grade three."

"Join the club." I snap my plastic fork in half with my thumb. "I can't believe Trish has her claws in him. Is there no justice in this world?"

"Not that I've found," Willa says, jamming her straw into her carton of chocolate milk. "So what's the fight du jour?"

"She keeps borrowing my clothes without asking. Got ketchup on my shirt. I've only worn it once."

"So borrow *her* stuff and trash it."

"She has terrible taste. I wouldn't be caught dead in her clothes."

"Even for the sake of payback?"

I shake my head. "Even for the sake of payback."

"She's going away to school next year, right?" Willa holds up both her hands, showing me her crossed fingers.

"Yup. She got early acceptance to Mount A. *Thank god.* They told her to apply for a scholarship because there was a good chance she'd get one." I hold up both my hands with my fingers crossed too. "It's kind of the only way she can afford to go. And trust me. Nobody wants her to go more than me."

Willa looks over at Trish's table again. "It's weird. She acts like a total airhead. You'd never know she was actually really smart."

"You got that right," I say flatly.

Just then we hear the voice of the principal, Mr. Scott, over the speakers. *"Attention, students, a few moments of your time please. Item number one, due to recent activities and the number of complaints after the fall semi-formal, Halifax West is no longer welcome at the World Trade and Convention Centre."*

The cafeteria erupts into a chorus of moans and groans.

"Also, due to recent activities and the number of complaints, the talent show scheduled for November 22nd has been postponed indefinitely."

More moans and groans, mixed with a couple of cheers.

"I'm guessing there's not that much talent at the West," I say.

Willa smirks. "Shocker."

"There goes our flute duet." I try to sound disappointed.

"And due to recent activities and the number of complaints, the cafeteria will no longer be serving the Cinnabon sticks with the icing dip."

The cafeteria immediately turns into a war zone.

"I bet it's because of all the disgusting things the football team does with that icing," Willa says. She twists around in her seat. "Sweet Jesus. You'd think it was the apocalypse."

"Apparently you can take away our semi-formals and our talent shows, but god help you if you deprive us of our Cinnabon sticks."

"Calm down! Everyone calm down!" Mr. Scott's voice booms over the speakers. He has a good view of the cafeteria from the glassed-in bulletproof office down the hall.

The cafeteria ladies come out, cross their arms, and stand in a line like the National Guard until order is restored.

"The school really should supply them with riot shields," I say.

"One last thing. Mr. Fraser will be holding a brief meeting at 12:50 for those band students interested in going on the January cultural and performance trip to New York. Thank you, and have a great day."

Willa ducks as a pizza crust whizzes by her head. "Come on. We should go to the band room *now*, so we can get a good seat."

"Definitely." I dump my wedges in the garbage and follow her into the hall. I'd been waiting for that announcement. Ever since we were told about it in that very first band class, it's pretty much all I've thought about.

"Mom's not going to let you go," a voice whispers close to my ear.

I spin around. Trish is walking right behind me. "You don't know. May—"

"Wake up and smell the latte, loser. It's going to cost like a bajillion dollars. You think Mom happens to have an extra shitload of money lying around that she doesn't know what to do with?"

My footsteps slow. I'd been so busy dreaming about Times Square, shopping, and Broadway shows, I hadn't really thought about having to actually *pay* for it. I just assumed Mom and I would figure something out. I mean, how much can it be? And I have *some* money saved already. Trish has a point though. There is no "extra." Like, we get by, but Mom has to work two jobs to make it happen. Did I expect her to start working three?

What was I thinking?

Guess I wasn't.

CHAPTER 2

WILLA NUDGES ME. "COME ON. SHE'S JUST BEING a bitch."

"Yeah, I know," I say sadly. "But she's right."

As more kids begin to pour out of the cafeteria, Willa steps between Trish and me. "Here. I'll deflect her evil rays."

I smile and let her steer me down the hall and away from Trish.

"You can't let her get to you," Willa adds.

"Too late." As usual, Trish has crushed my soul. And it's only lunchtime. What's she going to do with herself for the rest of the day?

"Let's not panic until we have an actual cost, okay?"

"Okay," I say.

When we get to the band room, it's already pretty full.

Abby Cameron is waving at us like crazy and pointing to a few empty chairs beside her. I pretend not to see and sweep my eyes up and down the aisles looking for any vacant spots—spots that aren't next to Abby. Abby is Trish's best friend. There's something about her that always seems to give me an immediate headache. She finally shouts my name out, making it impossible to go on ignoring her.

Willa screws her face up. "What's *her* deal? She usually doesn't even acknowledge our existence."

"Who knows?" I pull Willa along the row and plunk down in the seat next to Abby.

"Thanks," Abby whispers. "Todd asked me to save him a seat, but I'm sort of trying to avoid him."

There's no way I'm asking about her latest boyfriend drama, so I just nod sympathetically, turn to Willa, and start a fake conversation about how I'm boycotting Cineplex because they stopped giving out free refills on their large popcorn. Which isn't *completely* fake, because it's all true, and I'm totally pissed.

But Abby doesn't get the hint. "I think I'm going to break up with him," she says to the back of my head. "And, well… it's all about finding the right words, you know?"

I turn my body a bit more toward Willa and say loudly, "They didn't put up a sign or anything. They just said, 'Oh, we don't do that anymore.'"

Willa gives me a confused look. "Um. Yeah, I know. I was with you."

"It's not that Todd's not a great guy," Abby rambles on. "But he's going to university in Toronto next year, and I really don't see myself as the long-distance-relationship type."

Thankfully, Mr. Fraser stands and clears his throat. "Please, everyone take a seat, and thank you for coming.

Just a few things I want to touch on. Though much of our time will be spent performing with the other high school bands, there will be plenty of opportunity to enjoy what New York City has to offer."

"Oh my god. I'm so excited." Willa bounces up and down in her seat.

"Please note, people," Mr. Fraser continues, "the departure date of January 3rd. It overlaps with Christmas break, so adjust any family vacation plans accordingly. I have copies of the proposed itinerary here." He hands them to the kid sitting in the front row. "Pass it back, please."

He keeps on talking, but I'm not listening. I'm too busy reading the list of things planned. Four Broadway shows—we even get to vote on which ones—as well as the MoMA, the Met, and a whole day of shopping…

"…estimate the cost at $2,100 per student. Anyone interested, please review the attached payment schedule and deposit due date," Mr. Fraser says.

My head whips up. *What? That much?* $2,100…plus spending money…

"That's pretty cheap," Willa says. "I thought it'd be way more."

Mr. Fraser could have said $3,100, or even $4,100, and Willa's response would have been the same. She doesn't have much of a concept of money, which is a nice way of saying she's kind of spoiled. Willa's dad is a cardiac surgeon and her mom owns a chain of gourmet cupcake shops. But as if that isn't enough, they're also recently separated. The title for Parent Numero Uno is an ongoing battle.

And Willa knows how to work them.

"Cheap for you, maybe, but not for me." I rub my forehead. "I only have about $800 left from lifeguarding at the lake. I don't know why, but I just didn't think it would cost that much." Guess Willa's not the only one with no concept of money.

"But I can't go without *you*," Willa whines.

"It's okay," I lie. "Take lots of pictures. It'll be *almost* like I was there."

The meeting breaks up and people begin filtering out of the band room. Willa and I stay put. We just sit there, clutching our itineraries and staring at the wall.

"So what's the plan?" Willa finally says.

"Plan? The plan is you're going to New York and I'm going to wait for you to get back and tell me all about it. Oh yeah, and buy me a nice souvenir."

Willa shakes her head. "We've been best friends since grade one. I wasn't kidding. I'm not going without you."

"Unfortunately, I don't think you have much choice."

"Your mom will think of something. She always does. Remember when you wanted that dress for the grade nine grad?"

"Yeah...this is a little different."

"You know..." She taps a finger against her chin. "You could always ask her to sell her blood."

"True, true." I nod, all serious-like. "I mean, how much do you really use your blood, anyway?"

Willa laughs. "You know if my dad heard you, he'd go into some long lecture about blood and how it pumps through your veins carrying this, that, and the other thing—blah, blah, blah." She zones out for a second, then sighs. "I haven't seen him much lately. It sucks."

I reach over and give her hand a squeeze. Though Willa wants for nothing, has every whim fulfilled, I know she'd give it all up in a second if it meant her parents would get back together.

She returns the squeeze. "Why don't I just ask my parents for the money for you to go? They'd totally give it to me."

I stand, fold up the itinerary, and slide it into my back pocket. "Thanks, Willa, but no."

"Okay. What if it's a loan?"

"No. That won't work either."

She looks so crestfallen. Shouldn't that be me?

"Don't worry," I say. "I'm sure there's an answer out there somewhere."

Her face brightens a bit. "Yeah. Everything will work out."

The first bell rings, signalling seven minutes till class, and we head out of the band room.

"I have to go to my locker and get my art stuff," I say. "I'll see you after school at the bus stop, okay?"

"Okay." Willa walks backward down the hall. "Do you wanna come for supper?"

"Sure."

It's pretty much a regularly scheduled thing now. Willa's older brother, Sean, often works Thursday nights and Willa doesn't like eating dinner alone with her mom. She says it's too depressing.

Mom and I eat supper alone, just the two of us, all the time. Trish is usually MIA, which is fine by me. Less indigestion that way. But I know it's all new to Willa.

"We're having tacos. As usual!" Willa hollers just before she disappears around the corner.

In Art class I eavesdrop on a couple of girls sitting behind me. They both play clarinet and are quietly discussing the trip. From what they say, I can tell they have jobs—one works at Hollister, the other hostesses at East Side Mario's. They're trying to calculate how much they'll have to earn per week to cover the trip. I can't help feel a little jealous—okay, bitter. I've dropped my resumé at a bunch of places and haven't heard a word back. I perk up when I realize they've done the math wrong.

It's raining after school. I hold my knapsack over my head as I run to the bus stop. Willa is already there, pressed up against the outside of the bus shelter, trying to stay under the roof overhang. The shelter itself looks like it could burst open any second; a hundred—or at least twenty—students are crammed in like sardines. The glass is all steamy and dripping with their breath and body heat. Yuck. I'd rather stand in the rain.

At that moment, Trish drives by in Abby's car. They honk and wave as they pass. I notice the back seat is empty. "Useless trolls," I mutter.

"Remind me to ask Siri the best place to bury a dead body," Willa says.

I'm soaked by the time I schlep up my driveway. Trish and Abby are standing on the front porch. Trish is patting Abby's back and Abby's shoulders are shaking. She's crying. High probability it has something to do with Todd, but my desire for warmth and dry clothes trumps any curiosity I have. They both squeal as I bust them apart and red rover my way through their emotional barrier.

After I change into sweats and a hoodie, I go to the kitchen. I'm just finishing making hot chocolate when Trish comes in. "God, Lizzie. Could you be more of an asshole? Couldn't you see that Abby was upset?"

"Let me guess." I spoon a glob of Nutella into my mug. "They cancelled *Grey's Anatomy*."

She places her hands on her hips and curls her lip. "No. Todd dumped her. And *don't* joke about cancelling *Grey's Anatomy*!"

I roll my eyes. "So why's she crying? Wasn't she going to break up with him anyway?"

"Like *that* matters," Trish says.

"What you're saying is, she's just mad he beat her to it."

"No!" Trish scowls, all defensive. "It was the *way* he did it. He sent her a text!"

I mull this over. Even Abby deserves better than that. "Ouch."

"I mean, they went out for almost a *year*," she says. "He's such a total social moron."

I have to agree. Todd is kind of...*ew*. "Too bad he couldn't have hired a trained professional to break up for him."

"No kidding," Trish says, reaching for the Nutella. "Someone should start a business for idiots like him." She takes my spoon and starts eating right out of the jar. "It'd be a total cash cow."

And there it is.

I actually have to reach out and steady myself against the counter. What are the odds that the answer to all my problems would come straight from Trish's mouth?

CHAPTER 3

"**A**RE YOU SURE YOU'RE OKAY WITH TACOS AGAIN, Lizzie?" Willa's mom, Marlene, rips open a packet of seasoning and sprinkles it over the frying pan. "You must think that's all I know how to cook."

"I'd hardly call browning ground beef *cooking*," Willa says sarcastically.

Marlene's face goes all tense and her lips stretch into a thin line.

I shoot Willa a "What's wrong with you?" look, even though I know exactly what's wrong. She's convinced that her mom is the reason her dad left. "No, no. I love tacos, Marlene. We never have them at home, so this is great."

Marlene gives me a grateful smile before turning to Willa. "Get the sour cream and salsa from the fridge, please," she says coolly. "And don't forget Lizzie's guac."

I mentioned once that I liked guacamole, or maybe Marlene asked, I can't remember. Ever since, she always has it in the house for me.

Willa drags herself to the fridge. "I don't know how you can eat this stuff." She passes me the container. "It looks like puke."

Marlene violently bangs the wooden spoon on the side of the frying pan. "Let's eat," she says, trying to sound chipper.

At the table, I carry most of the conversation. I'm actually pretty good at it now. After the first couple of times eating in total silence, I knew there was no way I was living through that anymore. So one night I just decided to open my mouth and start talking. It helps that I have an endless supply of stupid stories about Trish.

Willa's only contribution is, "Wow, Mom. Cupcakes for dessert. *That's* original."

After dinner, Willa and I excuse ourselves to do homework. Well, I do. Willa just leaves. I'd been waiting until we were alone to share my news. I shove Willa's bedroom door closed with my butt. "Prepare yourself. I think I may have come up with a plan. Well…" I scrunch up my nose. "I can't believe I'm saying this, but Trish actually may have been the one who came up with the plan."

Willa looks up from her laptop, raising one eyebrow. *"Really?"*

"Long story short, Todd broke up with Abby via text. Then Trish said something like, someone should start a business—like, do the breaking up for them. You know, for those who lack the skills to do it properly."

"Hmmm." Willa considers this for a second.

"And, like, remember how Connor broke up with Lydia? He got his friend Ian to tell her."

Willa begins to nod. "There *are* a lot of losers out there."

"I prefer the term *socially challenged*."

She points a finger at me and winks. "That's because you're too nice."

"I don't know about that...."

"Stop. You know you are." She pulls her hair back, twists it into a knot, and stares intently into her laptop screen. "A business...a business...a breakup business.... Okay, let's start a list of things we have to do."

"We?"

"Yeah. We'll be partners."

"Why? You don't need the money."

"Don't you ever listen? I told you. I'm not going to New York without you. You have no business savvy. I, on the other hand"—she looks back at me over her shoulder and flashes me a dazzling smile—"am brilliant at everything I attempt. I will *ensure* your success."

My nose gets tingly. "Thanks, Willa."

"No worries. But my laptop's about to die. Is my cord on the floor?"

I sprawl across her bed, hang over the edge, and check around the carpet. "Nope."

"Must be in my knapsack."

I flip onto my back and listen to Willa rummage through her giant walk-in closet. "So we're going to start a business?" I say. "Just like that?"

"There's obviously a market, so it's not going to be too hard." Her voice sounds muffled and far away.

"And you think people are really going to hire us? To break up for them?"

"I guarantee it." Then there's a bang, a crash. "Oh, wait. Here."

Something hits me in the chest. "Ow!"

"Do you want that?" she asks, sticking her head out of the closet door.

I pick up the unidentified flying object. It's a purse. Coach. "What do you mean?"

"Mom got it for my birthday. I don't like the colour. Plus everyone and their dog has a Coach bag. I'm holding out for a Dooney & Bourke. Dad's going to Boston for a medical convention. He'll ask me if I want him to bring me back anything."

"So return the Coach one. Keep the money."

"Nah. It's probably past the return date."

I run my fingers over the bag. It's gorgeous. *I* could sell it. *I* could keep the money...for the trip...I hand it back to her. "Thanks, Willa, but I can't."

She shrugs. "Suit yourself." She chucks it into the back of her closet. Then she sits at her desk, plugs the cord into her laptop, and starts typing. "We'll need to advertise. Mom says her website is one of her most important business tools. And it's one way we can get the word out."

"Okay. That makes sense. But what should our thing be? Like, how do we carry out the deed, do the actual breaking up?" I tug on my bottom lip, concentrating. "Singing telegram? Poem? Letter? Gift?"

Willa's fingers go still. "No. It should involve chocolate. Chocolate makes everything better."

"Yeah, but as you know, I'm more of a Doritos kind of gal."

"Okay...then maybe it should be designed to each—what should we call them? *Victim*?"

"Well, there's no point beating around the bush. They *are* getting dumped. How about *dumpee*? The other person will be the dumper."

"Sure." She nods. "And so like I was saying, it should be designed to each dumpee's personal taste."

"We can use a basket, fill it with their favourite things as told to us by the dumper."

"That'll work," she says. "Next we need a name for our business."

We toss some ideas back and forth. Like *Breakups R Us, We Do Your Dirty Work, Time to Move On.*

"That last one sounds like a funeral home," I say.

"Okay. What about *The Enders*, or *The Destroyers...The Annihilators?*"

"They all sound so violent." I frown. "We're not trying to wreck anyone's life, we're just helping people say goodbye. Nicely."

"We could be *The See Ya Later Alligators.*"

I twist up my mouth. "*The Goodbyers?*"

"Nah." Willa shakes her head, then stops. "*The Goodbye Girls?*"

I repeat it a couple times to myself, roll it around my tongue. "I like it. Kind of glam and classy."

We start constructing the website. Willa really is brilliant at everything.

"We should offer different levels, like according to what people can afford," I suggest.

"That's a good idea. Say...silver, gold, and platinum?"

"Uh-huh. And they could pick depending on how much they care, or cared, about the person, or how long they went out."

"Or how guilty they feel," she adds.

I snap my fingers. "We'll have a questionnaire on the website that the dumper can fill out about the dumpee, likes and dislikes, that kind of thing. That's how we'll know exactly what to put in their basket."

Willa nods. "We'll work out the cost to us and decide what to charge from there. It should be at *least* double."

"It's the perfect plan," I say. "We should make a sort of 'suggested items' list for each package level and do an estimate so we can post the prices."

"Hopefully most will go for the platinum. Because people are going to talk, right? And no one will want to look like they cheaped out."

My eyes get big. "Of course. The backlash could be vicious."

We plunk ourselves down on her bed with a scribbler. First we decide on the questions for the questionnaire. Then we pick the things that will be common to all packages—favourite salty and sweet snacks, beverage (non-alcoholic), DVD, maybe a book, and definitely a blown-up headshot of the dumper, mounted on Styrofoam, with a set of darts. The higher-level packages will just have more things.

Willa wants to create a comment box where the dumper can write a personal message that we'll print off and include in a card. But I'm doubtful people will believe we won't read it even if we say we won't. Willa seems to think that they're not going to even care if we do. We argue about it for a while and in the end we choose to leave it up to the dumper—they can write one or not.

I scan our notes. "I bet we can get a lot of this stuff at Dollarama."

"And my cousin, Randy, works in the photo department at Walmart. He can totally hook us up with the headshots, probably have them mounted too," Willa says.

I stare back down at the notes. "If our math is right, we should charge forty bucks for silver, sixty for gold, and eighty for platinum. Sounds like an awful lot, doesn't it?"

"Are you kidding? I was selling lollipops the other day for a school fundraiser. You wouldn't believe how many kids whipped out fifties to pay for a two-dollar sucker. There are over fifteen hundred students at the West, and a ton of them have money. I say we go sixty, eighty, and a hundred."

I do the math quickly. We'll be making forty bucks' profit even on the cheapest baskets. But I'm still not so sure. "Willa?"

"Yeah?"

"Shouldn't we feel sort of bad about this? Like, making money off the misery of others?"

She looks at me like I'm crazy. "They'd break up whether we were on the scene or not. If anything, we're making it a nicer, more enjoyable experience for them. Actually, the more I think about it, we should probably be nominated for a Nobel Peace Prize."

I guess she has a point—though maybe not about the Nobel Peace Prize. "Okay. Since you put it like that."

There's a Taylor Swift calendar hanging above Willa's desk. She goes over and flicks through the pages. "About two and a half months. A little over ten weeks. If we pull off at least three or four breakups a week, that should totally cover your cost, and even spending money."

"No, Willa," I say firmly. "We have to split it evenly."

She sighs loudly. "Just calm down. Let's get you taken care of first, then we'll worry about me. Okay?"

I sigh too. "Fine."

"I'll make flyers to get the word out about the website," she says. "I'll print a bunch off tonight and we'll tape them up all over the school tomorrow."

Then something occurs to me. "Willa," I say. "Putting up the flyers. We can't be seen. We can't let anyone know it's us."

She frowns. "Why? I can't wait for everyone to know what amazing entrepreneurs we are."

"Don't you get it? Anyone in a relationship, if they see us coming toward them, will run screaming in the opposite direction."

"Well, we wouldn't do deliveries during school hours…." Willa chews on the tip of her pencil. "But you're right. They'll still avoid us like the plague."

"We're like those people at big companies who hand out pink slips that say you're fired."

"Or the Grim Reaper." She nods. "Okay. I'll make up an email account that's attached to the website. And we'll be real subtle about putting up the flyers. Maybe pick a time when the school's mostly empty."

"All right." I'm excited and nervous at the same time. "And you're sure no one will know it's us?"

"I'm sure," she says. "Trust me. Our plan is foolproof."

CHAPTER 4

MOM IS LEANING AGAINST THE KITCHEN COUNTER sipping her coffee. I glance at her sideways as I spread peanut butter on my bagel. There's something different about her. I sneak another look. Makeup. She's wearing makeup.

"Hey, Mom," I say. "You look nice."

At first she seems confused, like she doesn't understand my comment, but then she smiles. "Thanks, Lizzie."

"What's the occasion?"

"I think I just got tired of looking like I could haunt a house."

"You always look good, Mom," I say. "Especially for your age."

She raises her eyebrows. "Wow, thanks."

"You know what I mean." I smash my bagel halves together and press. The melty peanut butter oozes out the sides. "People are always saying how young you look."

Running a finger under her eye, she says, "Not many young people have the bags and dark circles that I have."

"That's because you work too much," I say, licking the globs of peanut butter off the edge of my bagel.

She shrugs. "It's all good." And she sets her mug in the sink.

In that second I see the exhaustion in her face that no amount of makeup can hide. Now's not the time to bring up the New York trip. I don't want to make her feel bad about saying, "We can't afford it." Of course, she's not going to *have* to afford it, but I'm not ready to explain all that to her yet. I'm not sure she's going to be totally on board with our business plan.

"Are you working at the gym today?" I ask.

"Yup."

"I thought you were only supposed to be part-time reception. You're there a lot more than part-time."

"That's fine. I'm not complaining."

"You never do, Mom. Maybe you should."

"And what?" She sweeps an arm through the air. "Risk depriving you of all this?"

"Ha, ha," I say and wrap my bagel in a piece of paper towel.

She gives me a playful nudge. "Can I drop you at school on my way?"

"That's okay. Willa and I are going in early to sort sheet music for band," I lie. "Her mom's picking me up."

"Willa's mom. How's she doing?"

"Um, I dunno. Okay, I guess."

It's weird Mom asked. Though Willa and I have been best friends forever, our moms never really got to know each other. They kind of travel in different circles. But I guess now they have something in common—singlehood. Maybe they'll become BFFs.

"It can't be easy, though," she says.

"Everyone has shit, right?"

She makes a face. She doesn't like it when I swear, but she can't really say much, because the stuff that comes out of her mouth, say like when we're driving in traffic, could peel your nail polish off.

"Anyhow," she says. "I picked up a shift at the bookstore. You and Trish will have to fend for yourselves for supper."

"We'll survive." I shove my breakfast-to-go into the front pouch of my knapsack. "Love ya," I say as I head out.

"Have a good day," she calls after me.

Willa's mom's car is pulling up to the curb when I step out onto the porch. I slip into the back seat. "Hey, Willa. Hey, Marlene. Thanks for coming to get me."

Willa grumbles some kind of response. Marlene gives me a tight smile in the rear-view mirror. I sit quietly and think about Mom, and how it's nice that she's taking an interest in herself and how she looks. Not that she needs to, but who knows? Maybe she'll meet someone. Dad's been gone for twelve years now. She's due.

A few minutes later Marlene pulls up in the school drop-off lane. "There you go, ladies."

"Thanks!" I say and scramble out the back.

"The housecoat's a nice touch, don't you think?" Willa says as she slams the car door shut.

"Sorry, what?"

"She's wearing her housecoat under her jacket. And her pyjamas!"

"Oh. Well, it's not like she's the only mom who's ever driven her kid to school in her PJs."

Willa glares at me. "I can't remember the last time I saw her in actual clothes."

"Calm down and cut her some slack. She could be a little out of sorts, what with all that's happened, you know, with your dad and stuff."

She doesn't say anything as we walk to the front entrance of the school.

"Getting dressed up might not be high on her list of priorities right now, that's all," I add.

"Yeah. Whatever."

Once in the foyer, aside from the janitor un-stacking chairs in the cafeteria, the school looks empty. The teachers are already here, but probably all in the teachers' lounge doing whatever it is they have to do—yoga, black magic, intravenous caffeine drip, a good old-fashioned game of Twister—to help them face another day at the West.

Wordlessly, we both peel off our jackets and tie them around our waists. Willa shifts her eyes one way up the hall then down the other. She gives me the all-clear nod, takes out a roll of tape, hands me a small stack of papers, and we get to work.

All posters, flyers, and notices are supposed to be approved and signed by the office. Ours are neither, so we have to be super ninja, sliding along walls and checking around every corner like we're CIA or something.

When we're down to the last flyer, I say, "I think I'll put this on the bulletin board outside the cafeteria."

"We finished just in time." She jerks her head toward the window. The parade of buses is starting to pull up in the bus loop. "I'm going to my locker. I'll see you later in English."

"Okay." I quickly put up the flyer and jam the tape into my back pocket just as clusters of kids begin to trickle in the front door. I step back to make sure I hung it straight when—

"Hey, Lizzie. You're here early."

Garret. I spin around. "Uh…" He's wearing his West varsity jacket. How does he always look so perfect? "Yeah…" I have to stall for a minute to pull myself together. My eyes drop. It's then that I notice a smear of peanut butter across the stomach of my sweater. *Sweet.* "I guess. A bit."

He smiles, possibly finding my loserliness adorable, and peers over my head. "What are you looking at? Did they post a date for the coffee house yet?"

"Uh…" I slap my hand over the congealed peanut butter. "Did you go to the band meeting about the trip?" I blurt. It's all I can think of to say. It's either that or "Can I touch your hair?"

"I had to rewrite a physics quiz. I heard about it though. Are you going?"

He's asking if I'm going. I have to swallow first. "I'd love to, but I dunno. It's a lot of money. Are you?"

"I'd like to…but there's Trish. She wouldn't be too keen on me going. You know, without her."

I frown. "You can't not go because of *her.*"

"Yeah, but I don't know if it'd be worth it. She'd be super ticked." He leans sideways, toward me. "You know how she can get."

Do I. God, there isn't a day that goes by that I don't pray some family will show up on our doorstep and say there was a mix-up at the hospital. We'll make the trade and I'll finally have my very own real human sister.

"Anyhow." He steps around me and toward the board.

"So is there anything—hey, what's this?" He's looking right at my flyer.

"Oh, that?" I squint and pretend to read the ad. "I don't know…I think it's just some silly—" It's too late. He's reciting the email address out loud.

"Genius!" he shouts.

I was not expecting that. "Genius? You think so?" I say, smoothing my hair with my hand. "Really?"

"Totally," he says, still looking at the flyer.

He does seem impressed. I'm beaming from ear to ear. I so badly want to reveal that *I'm* the genius. Well, 50 percent of the genius.

"Who do you think it is?" He tugs on his chin. "Like, who do you think is behind it?"

I shrug and try to look innocent.

He takes one last look at the flyer and laughs to himself. "Well, I guess I'll see you later." And he strides off down the hall.

In a matter of hours, every single flyer has been removed by school officials. But they were obviously up long enough, because by lunchtime, all anyone is talking about is the website, as well as its anonymous creators. *Who are they?* I hear it asked over and over again while I'm standing in line at the cafeteria. A half dozen names are tossed around. Of course, none of them are ours.

Willa has her laptop at school, but we can't risk anyone looking over our shoulders, so we wolf down our lunches and walk over to Starbucks to check our email. We already have six people wanting to hire us.

I'm blown away. "That was fast," I say. "Who knew?"

Willa gives me a smug smile. "*I* knew."

"Okay, smarty pants." I peel back the sippy tab on my skinny vanilla latte. "So what do we do next? Reply, right?"

"Yes, siree," she sings, but then her face clouds over. "I forgot about payment. How are they going to get the money to us?"

"Could we get them to e-transfer?"

She shakes her head. "I don't know about you, but my mom can go online and see my balance."

"Yeah. Mine too."

"And I'm not sure how thrilled my mom would be with our new business venture, especially after she sees what I got on my math test. It would just be easier to deal in cold, hard cash—less of a paper trail."

I flick the edge of my plastic coffee lid while I think about it. "They could mail it. We could get a post office box at Shoppers Drug Mart. It's close to school. It'd be easy for us to collect."

"Brilliant. We'll go there after school and see about renting one." Willa starts typing. "I'll just tell them payment details will follow."

I watch her fingers fly over the keyboard. When she's done, she clicks her laptop closed. "This is really going to work," she says.

I can't help thinking she might be right. "New York, New York, here we come."

CHAPTER 5

THE GOODBYE GIRLS HAS BEEN UP AND RUNNING for a couple of weeks now. People don't seem to care anymore who's behind it, just as long as someone's willing to do their dirty work for them.

We've successfully completed seven breakups—seven already!—and have a whole bunch more lined up. It's almost too easy. Even our transportation problem, which I had worried was going to be a major issue, miraculously solved itself.

Willa's older brother, Sean, is taking a year off after high school to, from what I can see, sit around the house playing video games. Luckily for us, for the bargain price of a Whopper combo meal, he's willing to do pretty much anything, including driving us around while he listens to his crappy emo music. He doesn't even ask what we're doing.

Because we don't want to be seen, all our drops have to be executed under the cloak of darkness. But we've got it down to a science. Sean takes us on a drive-by so we can check out the house and decide on the best approach. Then he lets us out a little ways away and we backtrack, mostly through wooded areas and neighbouring yards. We ring the doorbell or knock, run and hide behind the nearest shrubbery, parked car, or garbage bin, and spy until we see someone take the basket inside. It's really our only way of guaranteeing delivery. So far, there have only been a few tiny glitches.

Like, this one time a father-type answers. "Ellen. Call the tree guy!" he hollers back into the house. "Marg and Bill finally decided to apologize. That spruce is comin' down!"

Crouching in the darkness, Willa and I look at each other. "They'll figure it out," she whispers.

Another time, Lauren, a girl from my Drama class, opens the door. She looks down at the basket. She knows what it is, and immediately bursts into tears. A giant knot balls up inside my stomach. I watch her standing there sobbing for what feels like an hour. She slowly shuts the door without touching the basket.

Willa and I make our way back to the car in silence. As we settle into the back seat, Willa holds up a handful of mini chocolate bars—leftovers from Halloween. Her mom always buys too much. "I know that was brutal," she says, "but he would have broken up with her anyway."

I nod, but don't take any bars. I'm not hungry.

I notice Lauren isn't in Drama the next day.

Then there's Jordan Short. He's in grade twelve and he's one of Trish's friends. Well actually, he's Garret's friend, so really only Trish's through association. Therefore he escapes the label of *giant asshole*, a label I save for the majority of Trish's "close" friends. Anyhow, his locker is near mine, and he's pretty nice. We yuk it up sometimes between classes. He and this girl Kelly Mason have been going out since junior high. But then last week, Kelly hires us and is willing to pay top dollar.

Those few days before the impending breakup, I can't look Jordan in the eye. When he cracks some corny joke about an upcoming assembly, I force myself to laugh, though on the inside I feel a bit like crying. It's weird, knowing something about someone that they don't know themselves. He has no clue what's coming. And every time I pass Kelly in the hall all I want to do is scream, "Are you crazy?! You clueless cretin!"

The night we make the drop at Jordan's, he opens the door and looks up and down the street, then down at the basket. Even though the porch is dimly lit and we're across the street, I can see him frowning with confusion. After a few seconds, his face clears and it dawns on him. He picks up the basket and throws it against the garage door.

"There's a hundred bucks shot to hell," Willa whispers.

He isn't at school the next day either.

Over breakfast I finally tell Mom about the trip. I can't believe it's only two months away! It's not like I can wait until the week before and say, "Hey, by the way, I'm going to New York, but no worries, I have the two thousand bucks to cover it."

She sits at the kitchen table looking totally wiped, as usual. Now there's guilt and sadness mixed in there too. "You know I'd love to see you go, Lizzie, but there isn't—"

"It's okay, Mom. I'm going to look into the fundraising stuff they're setting up at school. Kids who went last year said you can really make a lot of money."

She presses her lips together and doesn't say anything.

"It can't hurt, right?" I say in a super positive voice.

Squeezing my hand, she smiles. "You're absolutely right. It can't hurt."

"Here's a wacky idea," Trish says sarcastically, hanging off the fridge door. "Get a job."

Mom sighs. "Trish. You know I'm not keen on you girls working during the school year. The money from your summer jobs should get you through. I want you to concentrate on your schoolwork."

"And I've tried to get a job, Trish," I point out. "You know I have." *In spite of Mom's wishes.*

Trish bats her eyelashes and mimics what I just said under her breath, of course loud enough for me to hear.

I shoot her my best death-ray glare. Then I turn my attention back to Mom, who's oblivious to what's going on behind her. "Willa's going to help me brainstorm too," I say. "And I think I've got some things I can sell online."

Mom gives my hand another squeeze. "That's a great idea."

I shovel in a mouthful of Shreddies. "I think this might be doable, Mom."

Trish is looking at me suspiciously from across the kitchen. I can tell her spidey senses are tingling. *Dammit.* I figured she might be a problem; that's why we set up shop at Willa's. I can't risk Trish snooping around my room, which I suspect she *totally* does. If she ever discovers what I'm up to, it'll be all over the school before the first bell, and my social life, or what little there is of it, will be non-existent.

Note to self. Keep an eye on Trish.

Jordan's back at school. Garret's leaning against the lockers talking to him. They look like they're having an intense conversation. I wonder if it's about Kelly and the breakup.

Do guys talk about stuff like that?

They both clam up as I get closer.

I jerk my head hello. I still can't seem to look Jordan in the eye.

Hiding behind my locker door, I try and jam all my junk inside. My Science textbook falls out twice.

I hear Jordan call out, "Catch you in Bio, bro," and Garret say, "Later, J Short."

The two-minute-warning bell rings and I dig out my English binder. When I close my locker, I see Garret sliding the side of his body along the wall of lockers until he's next to mine. "Trish here yet?" he asks.

He's wearing a light blue, button-down oxford shirt. It's the exact colour of his eyes. He should seriously consider wearing it every day. "She's got C block off, doesn't she? She's probably in the caf."

"Oh, right." He nods. "So, did you practice that new symphony yet?"

"No." *I've been too busy helping destroy people's lives for my own financial gain.* "I tried, but I couldn't keep my eyes open. Why does Mr. Fraser always pick such snoozefests?"

He laughs and watches me fiddle with my lock. He doesn't seem to be in any hurry to leave, not that I'm complaining. I try to think of something to say. "Uh…I heard Jordan and Kelly broke up."

"Yeah," he says. "He got one of those breakup baskets."

"Oh?" My voice cracks. "Did it…make it easier?" I know it didn't.

"Not really. Came out of nowhere. He's pretty messed up."

"That sucks."

"There was a dartboard in there with Kelly's face on it, though. He liked that. And beating the crap out of the DVD sort of helped."

The Hangover. When Kelly answered the questionnaire, she said it was his favourite. "I think he was supposed to *watch* the DVD, not beat the crap out of it."

He raises his eyebrows. "I don't think he was in the mood to watch a comedy."

"Yeah. I getcha." I start down the hall. Garret follows me. I turn, walking backward. "I guess everyone assumes it's only girls who get their hearts broken," I say. "But that's probably not true."

He shrugs and glances away, like maybe he shouldn't admit to anything.

"Guys maybe feel they have to hide it more," I add.

Garret gives me a funny look. "It's hard to believe you and Trish are sisters. You aren't alike at all."

I smile. "Thanks. That's the nicest thing anyone's ever said to me."

CHAPTER 6

MOM SLIDES THE NEWSPAPER ACROSS THE KITCHEN table. "I can't get the nine-letter word."

Spinning it around, I stare at the Word Target for a second. "Obtrusive."

She grabs the paper back, rolls it into a tube, and whacks me lightly on the head. "Show-off."

I shrug innocently and drain the milk from my cereal bowl.

Then—"Mom!"—the world's most annoying voice shouts from another part of the house. "Can you take me and Madison to the mall tonight?"

Mom sighs and doesn't answer. She has this thing about conversational yelling.

"It's like she's new here or something," I say, wiping milk off my chin.

"Mom!" Trish shouts again, louder.

We look at each other over the table and shake our heads.

Finally Trish shows herself. "Mom!" she huffs. "I've been talking to you."

Mom slowly turns in her chair. "That's not talking, that's screaming."

"God, Mom. I was getting dressed. You should be happy I'm multitasking."

"Oh," Mom says dryly, turning back around. "My apologies then."

"So can you?" Trish says.

"Can I what?"

Trish throws her arms in the air all dramatic. "Drop me and Madison at the mall."

Mom leaves her hanging as she takes her time flattening and smoothing out the newspaper and erasing a letter in the crossword. "No, I can't," she says. "I have plans."

This time it's Trish and I who look at each other. "Plans?" we both say at the same time.

Mom's head is down, studying the puzzle. "Yes. I'm meeting some…people after work."

"People." Trish frowns. "What people?"

"Don't you worry about it," Mom says.

Trish and I look at each other again over Mom's bent head and exchange words with our eyes. *Do you know anything? No, not a clue.*

"Well, like, where are you going?" Trish says.

Mom pushes out her chair and stands. "Trish, honey, as I said, don't you worry about it."

"Okay…" Trish shoots me one last look as she backs out of the kitchen. "Have fun, I guess."

"Yeah, you go, Mom," I say.

She smiles. "Thanks. There's money on top of the fridge for pizza."

In my room I pack my knapsack. From where I am I can see Trish standing in the bathroom brushing her teeth. I go and lean on the door frame. "It's good. About Mom. Don't you think?"

Trish, mouth full of foam, meets my eyes in the mirror and keeps on brushing.

I'm not sure why, but I sense Trish isn't as jazzed about the fact that Mom has plans as I am. "It is, Trish. It'll be good for her to go out, socialize with people."

She spits, slurps some water from the tap, and spits again. "Totally. Except she's not going out with *people*."

"What do you mean?" I say. "She said *people*. It's probably people from work."

"Trust me." Trish shakes her head. "I know the signs. It's singular. Person. Not people."

I roll my eyes. "You don't *know*. If it was a person, or like a *date*, why wouldn't she just say so?"

"Exactly."

Willa's standing on the sidewalk, waiting for me.

"Sorry I'm late," I say. "I was just talking to Trish."

"Those are words I don't hear often. Do tell."

"Nah." I don't feel like telling her about Mom. It'll only lead to Willa bashing her *own* mom, which sort of makes me uncomfortable. I really like her mom. "Not worth it. Trish doesn't even know what she's talking about."

"Yup. That sounds like Trish."

The trip deposit is due today, so just before we get to the bus stop, I pull Willa off the sidewalk and behind a clump of trees. "I took four hundred bucks out of the fund," I say, reaching into the side pouch of my knapsack. "Two hundred for you, two hundred for me."

She pats her jacket pocket. "Mom cut me a cheque this morning. It's all good."

"But half of this money is yours."

"Yeah, yeah. We'll divvy it up later."

I just look at her.

"Come on." She loops her arm through mine. "We have more important things to discuss."

The bus comes right away, so we don't get to discuss any of the "important" things she referred to. I can only assume it's about the business.

We drop our stuff at our lockers and head to the band room.

"We have to make up a schedule for the next couple days," Willa says quietly as we walk down the hall.

She's right. We're getting crazy busy. We've even received a few requests from other high schools. I told Willa we should decline, stick to the West, but she said that would be discrimination, and that if we service the neighbouring high schools the sky will be the limit. And Sean seemed okay with the extra travel. We just had to throw in dessert—a large Blizzard for any trips downtown or to Bedford.

Who knew there would be so many couples wanting to break up? I can't help but wonder if maybe there were a lot who were just hanging on, sticking it out, because they couldn't stomach the thought of ending it. Then shazam! We come along. The Goodbye Girls must seem like the answer to their prayers. Whatever the reason, we're reaping the benefits. We have three more breakups that have to be carried out before the weekend. Thursday and Friday are the most requested nights. Thursday because some want to be officially single by Friday. And Friday because some like the idea of not having to see the other person for two days. At least, that's what me and Willa think.

"I'll come over after school. We'll make a list of what we need," I say, joining the line of kids handing in their deposits in front of Mr. Fraser's desk. "And you should see if Sean is available Thursday after work."

"Believe me. He's available."

As I fish around in my knapsack for the cash, my elbow bumps the person in front of me. Before I can apologize, he turns. "Not you again."

How did I not notice he was standing right next to me? "Oh, hey, Garret." I'm surprised to see him. He'd basically said he wasn't going on the trip because of Trish.

"I changed my mind," he explains, as if reading my thoughts. "Like you said, I can't not go because of Trish."

Marvel. Someone actually listened to me. "Don't worry. Trish'll get over it."

"Yeah…." He doesn't sound very certain. Then he points to my handful of bills. "Trish told me you were planning on selling everything you own. Must be workin' for you."

I nod. "It's amazing what people will spend their money on."

The line slowly moves and it gets to my turn. I pay my deposit and Mr. Fraser hands me a receipt and a sheet of paper. "These are some fundraising ideas we've tried in the past. Feel free to participate in any or all. Any money you raise will come off of your own individual total."

"Thanks." I move off to the side to wait for Willa and read Mr. Fraser's handout. After she finishes she comes over and says, "I'm staying. I have to get Mr. Fraser to look at my flute. I'm having cork issues."

"Okay. I'm off to French."

"Wait. Did you see?" She waves Mr. Fraser's paper in the air. "A wake-a-thon. How awesome is that?"

I smile a smile that shows all my teeth. *Oh, I saw.* I'd rather donate half my brain to science. Going door-to-door begging for sponsors, then getting locked in a school gym with a hundred crazed, hormonal, sweaty high school students for twelve hours? *No thanks.*

"We *have* to go. It'll be so much fun. And because we don't really need the money, we'd only have to get a couple of sponsors, just enough to look like we made an effort. We could even make them up."

"Yeah…sure…maybe." I pretend to sound interested.

I basically run for the door like I'm being chased by a serial killer. One more second and I know she'll get me to pinkie swear or something.

For the second time I don't notice Garret, who's focused on reading the handout. We end up trying to squeeze through the door at the same time.

"Sorry," he says.

"Me too. I wasn't looking."

"Did you get one?" He offers me his handout.

"Yup. I'm good."

"So, wake-a-thon, huh?" His eyes are wide, his face beaming.

Oh no. Not him too. What is it about the wake-a-thon that brings this reaction out in people? "That's the word on the street."

"You have to go. They're amazing. I went to the one last year for the Brunswick Street Mission. They blast music all night, there's non-stop games, karaoke, they get us pizza—*for free.* It's a real easy way to raise some money. You *are* going, aren't you?"

My brain is screaming, "Please, god, kill me now!" But when I open my mouth, all that comes out is, "Of course I'm going."

CHAPTER 7

"**I**T'S OKAY, YOU CAN TELL ME THE TRUTH," WILLA says. "You *have* to be getting tired of tacos."

I shake my head. "I wasn't sick of them any other Thursday, why would I be sick of them this Thursday? Plus, we have them like once a year. Trish thinks she's a vegetarian."

"Is she seriously still sticking with that? Because I saw her at King of Donair last weekend. Eating a donair."

"Yeah...she doesn't count donair meat, pepperoni, or McDonald's cheeseburgers. She calls it 'selective vegetarianism.'"

Willa smirks. "Is *that* what she calls it."

We both laugh and huddle closer together against the cold as we trudge along the sidewalk.

We stop in at the library after school to do some homework. The business is taking over all our free time. I have tonnes of Math to catch up on and Willa has to write an essay for History due tomorrow. By the time we leave for home, the sun is hanging low in the sky, casting a purple-pink glow over the roof of the Canada Games Centre across the street.

"Why didn't I bring mitts?" Willa blows into her hands. "Let's stop at Tim's and grab a hot chocolate. My treat."

I'm about to decline, but I didn't bring mitts either and the thought of wrapping my fingers around a steaming cardboard cup is too tempting to turn down. "You talked me into it."

I pull open the door and breathe in the coffee-scented heat. While we stand in line, I stomp my boots and flex my fingers, trying to speed up the thawing process.

"Small hot chocolate," I say when it's my turn.

I hear Willa sigh behind me. She pushes me out of the way. "Two large hot chocolates and a sour cream doughnut, please." She looks back at me. "Want a doughnut?"

"No thanks, I'm good."

We pick up our order and are about to leave when Willa slows and elbows me in the side. She motions with her head to a table in the far corner. It's Trish and Garret.

I shrug. "Yeah, so?"

"Don't you wanna go say hi?" Willa asks, all coy.

"Oh, she'd *love* that."

She laughs and lets me manoeuvre her toward the door. But then she stops again. "No, wait. Watch. Something's definitely up."

I glance over at Trish and Garret's table. "Why? Wha… oh." I don't need to see Trish's face to know she's mad. I can tell by the way she's leaning over the table, the way her back is perfectly straight. She has one leg tucked up under her butt so she can get in closer. Her head is making little jerks up and down as she talks. She's talking a *lot*.

Me and Willa sort of hold our hot chocolates in front of our faces and shuffle sideways so we can spy from behind a display of packaged coffee and K-Cups.

Garret's eyes are cast down on the table. There's a tinge of red in his cheeks. He nods at something Trish says and shifts uncomfortably in his seat.

"I feel like we shouldn't be doing this," I whisper. "We should go." Before we get the chance, Trish and Garret push their chairs back and stand. They leave at the same time but through different exits.

"That can't be good," Willa says, taking a sip of her hot chocolate.

"He was probably telling her about the trip," I say. "He wasn't going to go. He said Trish wouldn't like it. I told him she'd be fine, that she'd get over it."

We're quiet on the walk to Willa's.

"You don't know if that's what they were fighting about," Willa finally says. "She could have been chewing him out for not holding her hand in the hall or some stupid thing."

"I guess," I say.

"And if they *were* fighting about the trip, it's not like it's *your* fault."

"I know."

"Oh, god. You don't feel guilty, do you?"

"No, no," I say.

"Or..." She gives me a sly look. "Maybe you're kinda happy?"

"No!" I punch her on the shoulder. She almost stumbles over the curb.

"Okay." She holds up her hand. "Simmer down." And she nurses her arm where I hit her for the rest of the way.

In Willa's front hallway, I throw my coat over the banister. She's about to do the same when I hear her suck in her breath.

"What?" I ask.

She's staring at something on the floor. I stand next to her so my line of sight is parallel to hers. I see a small red duffle bag beside a pair of men's sneakers.

"Dad's here." Willa whispers it like she's afraid to say it out loud. She beckons for me to follow her as she practically skips down the hall.

Then, "Marlene! Be reasonable!"

"Oh, go to hell!" Followed by the sound of glass breaking.

Willa stops short, which makes me smash right up against her back. Without speaking, we both turn and head upstairs to her room. A minute later the house vibrates with the slam of the front door.

"Would have been nice if he'd come up and said hi to his daughter, don't you think?" Willa says, her jaw clenched.

What do I say? "Yeah." I nod. "It would have been nice…but you never know, maybe he was late for something." Looking for a distraction, I pick up a roll of clear gift wrap from her desk and hand it to her. "Here. Let's do up these baskets. Pass me the lists."

She's staring off into space and doesn't answer me.

"Willa?" I say gently.

She snaps out of it. "Uh. Yeah. Sorry." She leafs through some stuff on her desk. "The lists, the lists…here we go." She holds up a piece of paper.

We get to work, lining the baskets with colourful straw, checking items off the list as we place them inside.

"I love the smell of this," I say, sniffing a candle before rolling it up in tissue paper. "I'm always surprised at some of the stuff people request."

Willa is folding the personal letters and sliding them into envelopes. "What does it matter at this point? Is the person getting dumped really going to care?"

I want to say, *Well, we hope so. It's kind of the point of our whole business*, but I don't. She's momentarily gone to the dark side. I can't really blame her.

As she drops the letters in each basket, she says, "You know, when I started high school, all I wanted was a boyfriend. I was so jealous of those gaggy, cute couples. How they'd hold hands, make out by their lockers. Now..." She gathers up the corners of the gift wrap on the first basket and scrunches it at the top. "I just feel sorry for them. They're all doomed to failure."

I cut off three strips of ribbon. "Not always," I say. Though I'm not sure how much I believe my own words.

Willa holds the wrapping tight while I tie bows on the baskets. Two pink. One blue. Two girls. One boy.

"I smell taco meat," Willa says. "Dinner must be ready."

Down in the kitchen, we find Marlene, her back to us, rummaging through a drawer and cursing under her breath. "Help yourself, ladies," she says without turning.

Willa puts two taco shells on a plate and passes it to me. "What did Dad want?" she asks Marlene.

Marlene is still rummaging. "Where is it?" she mutters. "Mom!"

"What do you want me to say, Willa?" She spins around. "That he was here because he wants to come home? Because he doesn't."

Willa folds her arms and stares at the cigarette dangling from Marlene's mouth. "You don't smoke," she accuses.

"I used to." Marlene flicks the lighter—the lost treasure from the drawer—and inhales deeply. "I quit for your father." She exhales, blasting out a stream of smoke. "But he doesn't live here anymore."

I stand awkwardly off to the side, waiting for some kind of cue from Willa.

She gives her mom a good glare. "We're eating in the family room." Then she takes her plate, stuffs her tacos with meat, and leaves the room.

I do the same, but shoot Marlene a weak smile as I grab the guacamole on the way out. She attempts to return the smile through a haze of smoke.

Sean is already there in the family room, planted on the couch watching *Coronation Street*.

"Since you got off early, can we leave by eight thirty?" Willa asks.

"Kay." He jams in a mouthful of taco. "I want one of those bacon-wrapped deep-dish pizzas from Little Caesars, though."

Willa rolls her eyes. "Fine."

We finish supper and set off to make our deliveries. The first two are routine, the baskets retrieved by an adult—a mom or dad. I like it best when it goes down that way; I don't have to see the faces or reactions of the dumpees. It still gives me an icky feeling, like something is curdling in my stomach.

I check the name and address for the last delivery. Heather Martin. "Do you know her?" I ask Willa.

She shakes her head. "I've heard the name before."

"I'm amazed at how many kids we don't know, though it's probably good. Makes it easier."

Willa quickly places the basket at Heather's front door, rings the bell, then joins me behind a pair of green bins.

We watch for a couple seconds and the door opens. Heather looks up and down the street first—they usually do—then she looks down at her feet. She bends to pick up the basket. I turn and start to crouch-crawl toward the street when I feel Willa grab my arm. "Check it out," she whispers. I contort my body and stick my head out around the green bin. Heather is sitting on the doorstep, the basket between her legs. She takes out random items and studies them under the porch light. She opens the scented candle, gives it a sniff, and smiles. Actually, she looks sort of happy. Finally she scoops everything up and goes inside. We hear her laughing as she closes the door.

"Well, *that's* a first," Willa says as we hurry back to the car.

I slide into the back seat. "I guess she really liked the stuff."

"She must have seen it coming."

"I wish more of them did," I say.

Willa talks me into going back to her place for a while. I should have gone straight home, but we hadn't finished doing up our shopping list for the next round of baskets and we were trying to stay on schedule.

We follow Sean into the family room. "Could you drive Lizzie home in about a half hour?" Willa asks.

"What the hell? We just got home," he whines, plunking down on the couch.

"Ummm…hold on," Willa says. She runs out then comes right back carrying a small brown paper bag. "There's a sour cream doughnut in it for ya."

It's the one she bought this afternoon with our hot chocolate. She must have forgotten to eat it.

He looks at the bag suspiciously. "Glazed?"

"Yup."

"Okay," he says, and she tosses him the bag.

"Wow," I say as we climb the stairs.

"He's very food-motivated. It's like training a puppy."

"Wow," I say again.

When we get to her room, Willa reaches for her notebook. "I like the scented candle idea. We should make that a standard item."

"Sure," I say. "Everyone loves a good scented candle. Even guys."

She nods and makes some notes. "I'm just going to double-check our email. I want to make sure we only have two due tomorrow, and none due the night of the wake-a-thon." She goes to her desk and starts up her laptop.

Crap. The damn wake-a-thon.

"Ha!" she blurts. "Mystery solved!" And she spins around the laptop so I can see.

There in the inbox is an order for a platinum breakup basket *from* Heather Martin. "Oh my god!" I say. "*She* was going to break up with *him*."

"See the time?" Willa points to the screen. "Tonight. 8:45 P.M."

"Little did she know, we were already en route to her house."

Willa nods. "Well, she doesn't need her order filled. We just saved her a hundred bucks."

"Plus, now she doesn't look like the bad guy." I smile. "Guess I'd be laughing too."

CHAPTER 8

I'M PRACTICING MY FLUTE WHEN MOM BRINGS IN A stack of clean laundry.

She waits and listens till I finish playing. "I meant to ask you," she says, setting the pile on the corner of my desk, "how was your dinner at Willa's?"

I frown. "Whaddaya mean? Like, how were the tacos?"

"No. More like, how are they doing."

I start taking my flute apart. "Okay, I guess. You asked me this before, Mom."

"I know. Aren't I allowed?"

"If you're so concerned, call up Marlene. I'm sure she could totally use a friend."

"No, no." Mom quickly shakes her head. "That would be weird. I barely know her."

I shrug. "She'd probably love a grown-up to talk to. They had a big fight the other night." I think of the whole cigarette thing. "I think she's sort of stressed."

"She and Willa had a fight?"

I nestle the flute parts into their velvet case. "No. Her and Greg, Willa's dad. He was there when we got home from school. It wasn't pretty."

"Oh," Mom whispers. "That's too bad. What was it about?"

"Not a clue. And Willa hasn't said anything about it since."

Mom sits down on the edge of my bed. "She's lucky to have a good friend like you, Lizzie. I know you'll be there for her if she *does* want to talk about it."

"Yeah," I say slowly. I can't figure out why Mom's all interested.

She must have read my mind, because she says, "It's just very sad when families break up." She stands and smoothes out the spot where she was sitting before leaving and closing the door behind her.

Still a little puzzled, I get up and put my clothes away. Is Mom comparing our situation to Willa's? Our family didn't break up. Dad died.

The only real similarity is that both our stories are sad.

"Do you have everything you need?" Mom asks, following me to the door.

"Yeah," I say, balling up my earphones and shoving them into my pocket. It's the night of the wake-a-thon, and I'm praying for some sort of natural disaster, zombie virus, or alien invasion—anything that might cancel it.

"And you're sure you don't want me to sponsor you?"

"No, I went door-to-door with Willa," I lie. "I got

enough." I hadn't wanted to ask Mom. I knew she'd feel she had to, so I'd made up a name, sponsored myself fifty bucks (that was the minimum needed to participate), and took it out of our business fund.

"Okay." She holds up a plastic grocery bag. "Here. I did up a bunch of snacks. Granola bars, rice cakes, dried banana chips—"

"Mom, they feed us there."

"I know. But it's going to be all junk. I want you to have something healthy." She shakes the bag at me as if somehow that'll make banana chips more enticing.

I stuff the bag in my knapsack. "Thanks."

"What about your pillow and sleeping bag?" she asks.

"Mom, it's a wake-a-thon. The keyword being *wake*."

"God. Why don't they have a sleep-a-thon?" Mom says, passing me my jacket. "Kids your age? You need your rest."

I smile and give her a hug. "I love ya, Mom. See you tomorrow."

Over her shoulder I see Trish standing on the stairs, a giant scowl on her face.

"I can't believe you guys are giving up a Saturday night to do this," she says. "It's so...*dorky*."

"What do you care? It doesn't affect *your* Saturday night." But I knew it did. Because Garret was going to be at the wake-a-thon.

"I *wish*. Student gov is donating all your food. I'm on the pizza-serving committee. And then, because I'm not a band geek, I have to leave."

"Well, why would you want to stay?" I keep playing dumb. "You just said it was dorky."

"Um." She tilts her head. "Garret's there." She says it like she's talking to a complete moron.

"Oh, woe is you."

"I don't know why he wants to go," she says. "He's going to die of boredom, stuck there all night." She drags her hands through her hair. "This stupid trip is ruining my life."

"Don't worry, Trish." I wink. "After you leave, I'll keep a close eye on him for you."

"Very funny," she snarls. "He only talks to you because you're my little sister."

Bitch.

Willa's mom drops us at the front entrance. "Don't forget to make good choices," she calls as we get out of the car.

"Mom. We're locked in the school," Willa says.

"I know. But it only takes a second—"

"See you at seven, Mom."

We walk toward the school door. A security guard is waiting and lets us in. On the way to the gym, we bump into Garret and some other band guys wheeling TVs on top of carts down the hall.

"What are you doing?" Willa asks.

"Oh, hey, guys," Garret says. "We're setting up a couple Wiis and a PlayStation in the gym."

"Sweet," Willa and I say at the same time.

Garret points at me with two fingers. "Care to have your ass kicked at Wii bowling?"

I raise my eyebrows. "FYI, I totally *own* at Wii bowling."

"Yeah, sure ya do," Garret laughs, and he and the other guys continue down the hall.

"What was *that?*" Willa says.

"What?"

"That. That little bit of somethin'-somethin'."

"I don't know what you're talking about."

"Frig off," she says. "You two were totally flirting."

I give her a shove. "*You* frig off. He's going out with my sister!"

"Yeah, *I* know that. But does he?"

Willa and I spend the first couple of hours wandering around the gym, talking to different groups of people, trading magazines, and watching some of the girls give each other manicures. Around ten o'clock, Mr. Fraser announces that the pizza has arrived and requests that we all give Student government a round of applause for donating the food.

Trish stands with the other members, smiling at the crowd, looking all, *No really, it's our pleasure.*

"Please," I whisper to myself.

I hang back while Willa goes up to get us some pizza. She comes back empty-handed. "Don't suppose you have anything to eat. The pizza looks disgusting. It's got little puddles of grease in all the pepperoni pieces, and it's starting to congeal and turn white." She makes a gagging noise.

"It's your lucky day. Right this way." She follows me over to the edge of the gym where all our stuff is. I take out the grocery bag from Mom and pass it to her.

She looks deep into the bag and squishes up her nose. "Tell me there are a bunch of chocolate bars hidden at the bottom."

"Yeah...probs not." I grab my water bottle from the side pouch of my knapsack. "I'm going to fill this up. You want me to do yours?"

She crunches on some banana chips. "Sure. These are a bit dry." She fake coughs and holds up her bottle.

"Water refill," I say to the teacher standing guard at the exit. She nods me through.

I go to the newly installed water bottle station and push on the lever. Nothing happens. "Perfect," I say. Luckily, there's a bathroom right across the hall.

When I pull open the door, there's Trish, sitting on the vanity, picking at her nail polish. "What are you still doing here?" I ask.

She looks up. "Waiting for Madison to come get me."

If I didn't know better, I'd say she'd been crying. I bend over and check under the row of stalls. All empty. "Are you okay?"

She sniffs and wipes her nose with her cuff. "Yeah."

"Because your eyes—"

"I'm *fine*," she barks, jumping to the floor.

I roll my eyes. "Okay…just thought I'd ask."

She stares at me for a second, like she's thinking hard about something. "Listen. You know how you said you were going to keep an eye on Garret?"

"That was a joke, Trish."

"Yeah, whatever. Well, I *want* you to keep an eye on him."

"What? Why?"

"Just to see if he's, like, paying extra attention to anyone, or if there's someone paying extra attention to him, that sort of thing."

"And what? Report back to you?" I shake my head. "I'm not going to be your spy."

"Shit, Lizzie. I'm not asking for your kidney. And I'd do it for *you*."

"Yeah right."

"I would," she insists. "That is, if you ever manage to get a boyfriend."

Bitch.

CHAPTER 9

*B*Y ONE O'CLOCK, THE GYM SMELLS LIKE THE BOYS' locker room.

Only six measly hours to go.

Willa and I are leaning against the wall, guzzling from our water bottles. We just finished an epic battle of Dance Dance Revolution. I have zero feeling left in my legs. But it was worth it. I was crowned champion, even though Garret tried to trip me so I'd lose to his friend Simon. After that major win, we moved on to Wii bowling, where I beat Garret about a half dozen times. My fist is still in a permanent clenched position from holding the remote so tightly. My body feels all rubbery and I have to keep curling and uncurling my fingers. I'd give my right arm for a pillow and a sleeping bag. Wish I'd listened to Mom. Can't let her know that, though.

Willa rests her head on my shoulder. "Whose genius idea was this?"

"Yours, I believe."

"You need to stand up to me more."

"Oh yeah," I say dryly. "That always works."

Without lifting her head, she raises her arm and flicks me on the cheek. "Smartass."

I drain my water bottle. "Your turn to refill. New bottle station isn't working, so just go to the bathroom by the caf." I think about my last trip to the bathroom and Trish's request. She had tried to hide it, but it was obvious she was upset. I scan the gym. "Have you seen Garret?"

"I think he's helping fix the laptop. It crapped out part-way through the Harry Potter marathon." She looks up at me and flutters her eyelashes. "Why?"

I wiggle her off my shoulder. "Trish wanted me to keep an eye on him."

She stands and puts her hands on her hips. "One, why does she want *you* to keep an eye on him? And two, and more importantly, why the hell would you do anything for her?"

"I know, I know. But I think she'd been crying. She asked me to see if he was, like, noticeably hanging out with some-one. I think she thinks he might be interested in someone else, or someone else is interested in *him*."

Willa closes her eyes and presses her fingers to her temples. "God, Lizzie. Sometimes you're so stunned."

"Hey! What's that supposed to mean?"

She snatches the water bottle from my hand and heads for the gym doors, shaking her head the whole way.

I cross my arms, set my jaw, and fume for a few min-utes. Oh, I know what she means. But she's way off—totally wrong. *She's* the one who's stunned, not me. And I plan on telling her that as soon as she gets back. Then my eyes widen. Somehow, from across the gym, I've made eye contact with Garret without even realizing it. So he probably saw my entire pissy mental rant about Willa as it flickered across my face. *God. Were my lips moving?* Which explains why he's looking at me with a sort of confused expression.

He's holding a coil of some kind of cord or wire in one hand and he gives me a hesitant wave with the other. I smile weakly and attempt a wave back. It turns out to be more of a limp hand flop. *This is all Willa's fault.*

"Are you two making googly eyes again?" Willa whispers in my ear.

"Would you stop it?!"

She sighs and passes me my bottle. "Oh, calm down."

"Because, like, I do *know* him, you know," I say defensively. "He's going out with my sister. It's not like we're not allowed to talk to each other."

"Talk your socks off." She chugs some water. "It's no skin off my nose."

"Yeah, well…" I mumble. "I—"

Willa cuts me off. "Check it out." She gestures with her head to a dark corner of the gym. We both watch as a guidance counsellor orders a boy and a girl out of a sleeping bag. There's a lot of frantic movement inside that sleeping bag before they finally unzip it. "Ah, trumpet players," Willa says. "Notorious for pushing the envelope."

I nudge her with my elbow and point to another part of the gym. "And apparently clarinettists."

Mr. Fraser has one of our clarinet players practically pinned up against the wall as he peels the lid off a Tim Horton's cup, sniffs, then drags the kid by the scruff of his neck out the exit doors.

"And Nathan was never seen again," Willa says.

"RIP, Nathan."

At that moment Katie, a fellow flutist, runs by and tugs on my arm. "Twister! Five minutes! Front of the gym!"

I turn to Willa. "I'm whipped. Let's take in some of the Harry Potter marathon."

"Sure. Plus it's dark down there. Maybe we can close our eyes for a bit and no one will notice."

We start toward the far end of the gym until Garret blocks our path. "Just who I was looking for. I need you guys for Twister."

"Uh…" I scratch the back of my neck.

"Actually," Willa pipes up, "we're kind of fried. We were going to chill for a while and watch some HP."

"Oh, come on, pleeease?" he fake begs, clasping his hands together. "We only need a few more people."

"Well…" I glance over at Willa. "Maybe one short game?"

Willa stares at me with bulging eyes. "Sure, Garret." She spits out the T.

"Yes!" He pumps his fist in the air.

"Just give us a sec," I tell him. "We'll be right over."

"Okay. But no chickening out," he says as he jogs backwards, flapping his arms like chicken wings.

"Maybe one short game, Garret." Willa does her best impression of me. "Anything for *you*, Garret." Then she makes kissy noises.

"Oh, shut up. It's a chance for me to do some recon for Trish."

"And again I'll ask, *why*? She treats you like shit."

I sigh, then go over and grab my knapsack. "We should go slather on some deodorant and brush our teeth. It *is* Twister, after all."

The game is intense. It's down to me, Garret, and our tuba player, Allan.

Willa messed up on the first round. But I know it was on purpose. She and I took gymnastics all through elementary. She's way more bendy than I am.

The spinner shouts. "Left foot green!"

Uh-oh. It's Allan's move and he's twice my size. He's partly arched over my upper body and if he loses his balance, he'll squash me like a bug. I squeeze my eyes shut and hold my breath, praying for it to be over.

Allan must sense my terror. "I'm out!" he yells and lurches himself away.

I start breathing again.

"Left hand yellow!"

It's my turn. I study the mat and try to figure out how to make the move. The only way I can pull it off will put me directly on top of Garret…like, face to face. I should just cave, but my desire to win takes over. I can do this.

I twist myself around and slap my left hand on a yellow circle. My head hovers over Garret, who's struggling to hold his crab pose. Our lips are only centimetres apart. I try to turn, but my shoulder is in the way. *Thank god I brushed my teeth.* My arm starts trembling. I can't hold the position much longer. Sweat makes my hand slip a bit on the plastic and brings me even closer to Garret—so close I can see the tiny blood vessels in the whites of his blue, blue eyes. *What's taking so long? Yell out the next move!*

I can feel the heat of the crowd pressing in closer around us. The spinner is dragging it out on purpose, trying to torture us. My arm starts to tremble more violently and my wrist finally gives out. I collapse on Garret's chest. Gasping, I flip myself off him as quickly as I can, as if he's on fire.

Allan yanks Garret up and all the guys start cheering and high-fiving.

"God." Willa throws her arm across my shoulders. "It's not like he split the atom."

I wipe the sweat off my forehead with the sleeve of my T-shirt. "Time for some Harry Potter."

Garret runs up to me, his hand extended. "Good match, Turner. You're a worthy opponent."

"Foiled by my own weak wrist," I say, grasping his hand and giving it a shake.

"Garret! Come on!" one of the guys calls out.

"See you later?" Garret says.

"You bet," Willa answers for me and pulls me toward the movie-viewing part of the gym.

On our way we pass by a couple having an argument. The girl keeps sweeping a finger under her eye. I think she's wiping away tears.

"That's the third couple I've seen fighting tonight," Willa says.

"Must be the dim lighting and lack of personal space. It's like it magically creates drama."

"The no sleep thing doesn't help. People get delirious. But whatever it is, we should anticipate a new batch of emails by Monday morning."

I dig my teeth into my bottom lip. "You might be right."

They're halfway through the third Harry Potter when we pick our spots, slide our backs down the wall, and sit.

I must have zoned out at some point because suddenly I notice Garret is beside me. He's stretched out, his head resting on his knapsack, eyes closed. I poke him on the shoulder. "Wake up," I whisper.

"I'm not asleep, I'm just resting my eyes." He pulls himself upright and stays for the end of Harry Potter three and all of number four. He's sitting so close our shoulders are touching. I can feel the heat from his body.

As the credits roll for *Goblet of Fire,* Mr. Fraser stands in the centre of the gym with a stopwatch and we all count down from ten to zero—it's finally seven.

Garret stands and stretches. "You guys need a drive?"

"No, we're good, thanks," Willa says.

"Kay, see ya," he says.

We both nod. "Yup."

The principal and a few teachers are standing in the front entry by a table with juice, hot chocolate, and boxes of granola bars.

"Want something?" Willa asks.

"Nah." My head is starting to throb. All my energy is focused on getting home to my bed.

When we push through the front doors, the sun is just starting to rise.

A horn honks. It's Marlene. She's fourth in a long line of parents waiting to pick up their kids. We make our way over to the car.

"Soooo," Willa says. "What are you going to tell Trish about Garret?"

I shrug. "That I didn't notice him with anyone, or anyone hanging off him. And that she doesn't have anything to worry about."

Willa opens her mouth then closes it. After a second she says, "Yeah. That's what I'd tell her too."

CHAPTER 10

I DON'T MAKE IT TO MY BED—THE STAIRS ARE TOO much to contemplate at the moment. I end up doing a face plant on the living room sofa. With my one exposed eye, I see a pair of shiny black high-heeled shoes standing neatly in the front hallway. I know they're not Trish's; she'd never take the time to line them up like that. So they must be…Mom's? *Mom doesn't wear shoes like that.* And then I drift off to sleep.

"Ouch! What the—?" I instinctively wave my arms around in the air.

"Shush," Trish says. "You'll wake up Mom."

I push myself up into sitting position. "Well, maybe if you didn't stab me in my sleep." I rub my upper arm.

"Oh, quit being such a baby. I only poked you."

I shove the hair back from my eyes and blink a few times. "What time is it?"

"A little after eleven."

I blink a few more times. "And Mom isn't up yet?"

"Never mind about Mom," Trish says. "Tell me—"

"Are you coming or going?" I interrupt. I notice she has her jacket on.

She throws her head back in frustration. "I slept over at Madison's," she says. "So...what's the update?"

My brain is still foggy. "What?"

"Are you being stupid on purpose? I'm talking about Garret." She spits out the T just like Willa did.

A bit more awake, I squint at her. "*That's* really gonna make me tell you anything."

She sucks in her breath. "So there's something to tell me?" She makes a fist. "I *knew* it!"

I rub my eyes. I could really have a lot of fun here...if I wasn't still half asleep. "No, there's nothing to tell you. He spent most of the night organizing games and stuff. And when he wasn't, he was just hanging out with me and Willa."

She closes her eyes and breathes in deeply. "Thank god."

Then she sits there without moving. Curious, I say, "Were you *really* worried?"

It takes her a few seconds to answer. "I'm not always so nice to him, you know?"

I nod. *Yeah, I can only imagine.* But I don't say it out loud.

"It's how I've always treated *other* guys. I guess because I knew I could get away with it, because I knew they liked me more than I liked them."

I nod again.

"Garret's different. I may have pushed him a little too far." She stares off into space for a second. "I think I like him more than he likes me. That's a first for me."

"Well…."

"I'm saving up to buy him a Fossil watch for Christmas." She looks at me. "I've never spent serious money on a guy before."

"You could maybe be a little nicer to him?"

It's like she suddenly remembers who she's talking to. "Are you really trying to give me relationship advice?" She stands up before I have a chance to answer. "Because I hope you know we would have to be living in some kind of parallel universe before I'd ever take it." She stomps off toward the stairs mumbling, "God, I can't believe I told you any of that. What was I thinking?"

No "thank you," no nothing. *Surprise, surprise.*

I lie back down and close my eyes. *Bitch.*

The smell of peanut butter pulls me out of a deep sleep. Mom is sitting on the edge of the coffee table holding a plate of toast under my nose. "Rise and shine, princess," she says. "It's almost one thirty."

I raise myself up onto my elbows. "Really?" I check my phone as if I don't believe her. "Crap. Half my Sunday, gone."

"Or half your Sunday still left." She smiles and passes me the plate. "How was the wake-a-thon?"

"Tiring." I peel the crust off a piece of toast. I can see that the high-heeled shoes are gone. "So how was your night?"

"Fine," she says, getting up and re-fluffing the sofa cushions.

"Because there was a pair of *fancy* shoes in the hall when I came home," I say slyly.

She keeps arranging the cushions.

I take another bite. "Yours?"

She hesitates, then says, "Yup."

"Ooooh, Mom. Hot date?"

Her cheeks turn a little pink. "Hardly."

"It's okay, Mom. You're old enough to date now."

"Ha, ha." She sits beside me. "You and Trish were away for the night, and I got…invited out."

"On a date," I say, hoping for confirmation.

She shrugs.

"So you're 'seeing' someone?" I air quote.

She looks down at her hands folded on her lap. "It's complicated."

"Let me guess." I lick some peanut butter off my finger. "Kids? Tonnes of baggage?"

She nods. "You could say that."

Just then my phone chirps. It's a text from Willa: Meet me at McDonald's asap. I can tell by the shortness of the message and lack of emojis that it's important.

I give Mom a quick pat on her shoulder. "I hope it works out for you, Mom. You know, if you want it to." I tug my hoodie over my head. "I gotta go."

"Where?"

"I have to go to meet Willa at McDonald's."

"But you just ate."

"I need ice cream," I say—the universal explanation.

Willa's already there, sitting at a table by the window and eating fries. Her laptop is open in front of her.

She doesn't look up as I sit down. "We *might* have a problem," she says. "More than one, actually."

Uh-oh. "Like what?"

"This morning after we dropped you off, we picked up Grace Munro. She was walking home from the wake-a-thon."

"And?"

"I don't know how it came up, but somehow we got around to talking about Rachel Currie. Ring a bell?"

"Rachel Currie…we delivered a basket to her last week."

"Well, apparently she dropped out of the wake-a-thon because she was so upset."

I start to get a bad feeling. "How do you know? Is she Grace's friend?"

Willa shakes her head. "I wish. Grace overheard Mr. Scott talking to Mrs. Fitzgerald. She said he was saying something about the baskets. Something like adding flames to the fire. He was going to make it a priority to find out who's behind them."

Dammit. "How does he even know about them?"

"He's probably heard talk. You know how he's always lurking around the halls. Plus he probably saw the posters." She rips the top off a salt packet. "Why does he even care? I mean seriously, students are upset about stuff all the time, so unless someone *complains*…doesn't he have bigger fish to fry?"

"It's going to turn out to be a school policy issue or something. Especially if he thinks somehow we're doing it through the school. Even though we're not," I add.

"He doesn't have a leg to stand on. The only connection to the school is that so far the majority of our customers are West students." Her eyebrows scrunch together. "I suppose he might have figured out it started up at the West, but I don't think we have to get hysterical or anything. It's just something we should keep an eye and ear open for. The last thing we need is him stickin' his nose in."

Tiny prickles of sweat bubble underneath my bangs. "So what's the other problem?"

"Well, it's not really a problem for me, but it might be for you."

I frown. "Okay…care to elaborate?"

She leans back in her chair. "When I woke up, I checked our email."

"Yeah?"

"Actually, I don't even know why I'm surprised. I knew it was coming."

"Knew *what* was coming?"

She pauses dramatically. I want to punch her.

"An email from Garret," she finally says.

"An email from Garret," I repeat. "An email about what?"

She snaps her fingers in front of my face. "What do you think, Einstein? He wants to order a basket for Trish!"

"*What?*" I check behind me, over both shoulders. "A breakup basket?" I whisper.

"No, an Easter basket," she says sarcastically. "Of course a breakup basket!"

I can only stare back at her. My heart is doing this weird fluttery thing.

She starts typing. "I'm sending him a confirmation."

I grab her arm. "No!"

She yanks it back. "Yes! We can't just randomly turn down a job."

"But she's saving for a Fossil watch."

"Yeah…" She shakes her head and returns to the keyboard. "I don't know what that means."

"It means she really likes him. She's going to be totally blindsided."

"They usually are," Willa says.

"Can't we say no just this one time?"

"We don't get to pick and choose who we take on."

"Why not?" I whine.

"Because that's not how you run a successful business," she says, then she stretches her body across the table toward me. "Plus, it helps keep our identities safe. Who would ever suspect one sister of aiding in the destruction another sister's happiness?"

My eyes widen in horror.

"Relax. It was a joke." She tilts her head. "Sort of."

"*Not* funny."

"Could you please find your chill? This is me you're talking to. You can be a little happy. I know you like him."

I feel the heat creep up my neck. "For the hundredth time, I do not!"

She jams a fry into the ketchup cup and pops it in her mouth. "Just because you say something a hundred times doesn't make it true."

CHAPTER 11

MY BODY FEELS LIKE TOTAL DEAD WEIGHT, BUT MY mind is full-on wide awake so I can't sleep. I did try to nap after I got home from meeting with Willa. It was useless. I finally give up and drag myself, draped in my duvet, down the stairs. There's a note on the hall table from Mom saying she's gone to work and giving detailed instructions for baking the shepherd's pie for supper.

I plunk myself on the sofa and stare blankly at the TV. There's an episode of *Big Bang* on. When is there not? The dryer hums from the basement and I have to turn up the volume. *Is Trish doing laundry?* I think for a second. *No, that can't be right.*

A few minutes later, Trish appears and stands between me and the TV. She shakes out a red sweater and holds it up. "Does this look like it needs to be ironed?"

My mouth falls open. "That's *mine*! And it's not supposed to go in the dryer! *Or* be ironed!"

"Relax," she says. "I took it out before it was completely dry."

"So?!" I stretch out my arm and try to grab it from her.

She whips it back, just out of my reach. "You never wear it, and Garret told me to wear something red."

My arm turns limp and drops to my lap. "Garret?"

"Um, *yeah*." She gives me that oh-so-familiar look, the one that implies I'm a complete moron. "We're going to a Moosehead game tonight."

"With each other?"

"Actually, we're going with Mr. and Mrs. Claus," she says all snotty as she pulls my sweater on over her tank top and flicks her hair out of the neckline. "Personally, I don't give a damn about hockey, but he's so crazed about it, I figured it wouldn't kill me to make an effort, right?"

Then something flickers in my memory. Something about her buying those tickets for Garret's birthday. *How could he still go?*

"You look like you're having a seizure or something," Trish says.

I swallow. "Isn't he tired?"

She raises her eyebrows. "From the wake-a-thon? He was probably bored stupid. I bet he slept through most of it."

I don't comment. I have that same icky feeling I had with Jordan. I know things about her that she doesn't know, things I *shouldn't* know. What makes it worse is the whole "making an effort" thing, like she's trying to nurture the relationship. It's *so* not like her. Maybe she suspects? I start to panic that she can see it in my face. "Mom went on a date last night," I blurt.

Trish picks a piece of lint off my sweater. "I know. I forgot the cheque for the wake-a-thon pizza and had to come back. I saw her leaving."

"Did someone pick her up?"

"No. She took the car."

I tug on my lower lip. "Sketchy."

"She told me it was complicated or something."

"Yeah. That's what she told me too."

Trish shrugs. "Actually, I hope she's just hooking up with someone."

Ew. I can't deny it. The thought of Mom hooking up makes me a little squeamish. "Why? Why would you want that?"

"Are you kidding? What if we had to merge with some random family? Had to live with some psycho wannabe dad and his loser kids? "

"Oh my god, Trish. That's not going to happen."

She juts out her chin. "You don't know that."

Before I can argue, a horn beeps from outside.

"That's Garret." Trish grabs her jacket off the chair. "I'm outta here."

"Have fun," I say after she leaves. And I actually mean it. *It's probably your last date. With Garret, anyway.*

The icky feeling lingers in my stomach. Then I realize that after all that, Trish never even asked to borrow my sweater. She just pranced off with it like she owned it. The feeling lessens.

My phone starts to ring. I root around in my crumpled duvet until I find it. It's Willa. She never calls. She only texts. "What's wrong?" I ask quickly.

"Calm down," she says. "I'm too tired to text, that's all."

There's something in her voice, something more than tiredness. "Are you sure you're okay?"

She pauses. "Dad was just here."

Sometimes that's good, sometimes that's bad. "Oh?"

"After the mandatory kitchen fight with Mom, he left with Sean. They went to the Moosehead game."

"You didn't go?" Willa loves the Mooseheads. Her family has season tickets.

"He asked. I declined." I hear her sigh. "I don't feel like being around him right now."

Confused, I say, "But I thought you were mad at your mom. You said it was all her fault."

"Yeah…I'm pretty much mad at everyone."

We don't talk for a bit. The theme from *Big Bang* drones through Willa's phone as well.

Willa finally speaks. "I heard Mom talking to Aunt Meredith. She thinks Dad's going through some mid-life crisis."

"It's possible, I guess. I'm not sure I really know what that is though."

"Me neither. Mom told her he's working out all the time, has a bunch of new clothes, says he's acting like a *teenager*."

I can't think of what to say to make it better, so I don't say anything.

"Sometimes I debate the pros and cons of running away," she says.

I sit up straight. "No, Willa."

"Don't worry, the cons always win out. I think it would involve a lot of work, maybe even some hardships. We all know I'm not cut out for any of those."

Relieved, I smile. "Speaking of the Mooseheads." I decide it's time to change the subject. "Trish just left with Garret for the same game."

There's a rustling sound, like maybe she dropped her phone. "*What?*"

"She bought the tickets a while ago," I explain.

"Oh, okay. I suppose he'd still go. It would be a kind of awkward date, though...love to be a fly on the wall."

"I don't know." I shake my head. "I don't think he should have gone. He *is* breaking up with her."

"Well...technically, *we're* breaking up with her. He hired us to do it for him so he wouldn't have to, remember?"

I'm still shaking my head. "All he had to do was say he was too tired from the wake-a-thon or something."

"The guy's not an idiot! They're playing Quebec. The game's sold out." She pauses. "It's okay if you're jealous. I totally don't blame you."

"I'm not!"

"Then what's your problem?"

"I don't have a..." My voice falters. "I dunno."

I can hear Willa tapping her fingernail against the phone. "Are you sure you're not feeling guilty because you know he likes you too, and you're kinda the cause of this? Not that it's your fault or anything," she adds. "The heart wants what it wants and all that crap."

My teeth clamp together. "*Wow*, Willa! That makes me feel tonnes better."

"Well, I know you *can't* be feeling sorry for Trish. She's like the biggest bitch on the face of the planet."

I draw in a deep breath then let it out slowly. I hate to admit it, but everything Willa says has a hint of truth. Maybe I *am* jealous, a little bit, because maybe I do like Garret, a little bit, so I guess I do feel guilty, a little bit, and Trish *is* a bitch—no little bit about that. I can't let Willa know that she's right, though. "You can't call Trish a bitch," I say sulkily. "Only I can."

"Fine," she says. "But I don't know why you just can't sit back and enjoy the show. No one deserves this more than Trish."

"No one deserves to get their heart broken." At that moment the timer on the dryer goes off, buzzing loudly. She didn't bother to turn it off when she took out my sweater.

"Even Trish," I finish weakly.

CHAPTER 12

I READ THROUGH THE QUESTIONNAIRE THAT Garret filled out for Trish's breakup basket.

"Oh no," I say. "Trish's favourite movie is *Love Actually*. He wants us to get it for her."

"So?" Willa asks.

"That's *my* favourite movie. Now it's, like, tainted or something."

Willa rolls her eyes. "There's loads of British movies out there with basically the same cast. You'll find a new favourite."

"Yeah right," I grumble.

"Lizzie. You've got to get a grip. It's not like Garret's the only guy that's ever going to break up with Trish. Are you going to be like this every time? Trust me, she's going to get dumped by a lot, and I mean *a lot*, of guys."

"That's not very nice."

She gives me a fake sweet smile. "I'm just sayin' it's going to take a real unique individual to put up with Trish's shit, long term."

I sigh and reach for the questionnaire. "Let's just get back to business."

Once we go over all of Garret's answers and requests, we make up our list and decide to pick up everything after school.

"We'll make the drop tomorrow night," Willa says.

"To my house," I say glumly.

"Yes, well, unfortunately that's where Trish happens to live."

I look at her.

"Oh, buck up." She punches my arm. "We'll buy her the anniversary edition DVD if it'll make you feel better."

"Thanks a bunch," I say.

Sean drives us to Walmart and waits across the street at Subway while we do our shopping.

The collector's edition of *Love Actually* ends up costing more than double the regular edition. I hold it back at the cash register to pay for it out of my own pocket.

"You're crazy." Willa grabs it from my hand and adds it to the pile the clerk is ringing through. "We've got loads of money."

I grab it back. "No. I want to buy it."

She mashes her lips together and shakes her head.

Trish sits across from me at the kitchen table picking all the nut clusters out of the cereal box.

Normally I'd wrestle it from her hand, or at least *try*, which would inevitably result in a giant screaming match, but this morning I just let her have at 'er and quietly wait until she's finished.

When she finally sets the box down, I pick it up and pour a bowlful of flakes, just flakes. No wait, I see one or two nut clusters in there.

Then Mom comes in singing a Taylor Swift song under her breath. She has the lyrics all wrong, but I give her an A for effort. Trish and I exchange glances.

"Mom," I say, "you're in a good mood."

She frowns and looks up at the ceiling, like she's thinking hard. "Yeah. I guess I am."

"Um, Mom," Trish says. "Is that my scarf?"

She looks like she's thinking again. "Yeah. I guess it is."

Trish opens her mouth to say something but Mom cuts her off. "You don't mind, do you? I think you actually still owe me for it."

Trish closes her mouth.

"Are you working today?" I ask.

"No." She pours a cup of coffee and avoids eye contact. "I've got a bunch of errands to do."

I look over at Trish and raise my eyebrows.

"Alone?" Trish says.

Mom taps her spoon against the edge of her mug, then she sort of smiles. "Fine. You got me. Not alone."

"You don't have to keep it a secret," I say, pouring milk into my bowl.

"Him," Trish corrects. "*Him* a secret."

Mom gives us another sort-of smile. "I'm just not ready yet." I see her swallow. "It's too soon."

"God, Mom. It's not like we're children," Trish says. "I think we can probably handle meeting some new guy."

Mom blows on her coffee and doesn't answer.

I'm waiting at the bus stop with one knee on the sidewalk, looking through my knapsack for my phone. There are a couple of girls right behind me giggling and shrieking like five-year-olds. I'm just about to jam in my earphones, when: "Did you hear? Jessie Mason got one of those breakup baskets the other night."

I steal a glance over my shoulder. They're minions of Trish's, but I can't remember their names. All her friends look the same—Kardashian wannabes.

"Lucky bum," minion number one says.

I tilt my head. *Did she really just say that?* I try to edge closer to them for maximum eavesdropping.

"How can you say that?" minion number two says.

"Oh, don't get me wrong. I'm sure it was awful, and I totally feel for her. It's just that, well…I've been waiting for ages."

"Waiting for what?"

"A breakup basket."

My jaw drops. *Is she for real?*

"Why would you—"

"Logan and I have been going out for like *ever*," minion number one says. "But lately all we do is fight. We're miserable! I know it's mutual, that we both want to break up, but nobody wants to be the one to spend the money."

"You don't *have* to use The Goodbye Girls," minion number two says. "Why don't you just break up with him face-to-face?"

"No way. It'd be so embarrassing to break up and not even get a basket out of it. I *want* my basket!"

I'm having a hard time getting my head around this conversation. I'm not sure how I should feel about it.

"I'm actually going out of my way to be a superbitch," minion number one continues, "hoping I'll push him over the edge. He works part-time at Sobeys. He can afford it way more than I can."

Then the bus pulls up.

"I hope it works out for you," minion number two says as we all move in a clump toward the bus doors.

"And I'll be so pissed if he cheaps out and doesn't get me the platinum package," minion number one adds.

I flash my bus pass at the driver and take a seat far, far away from them. I sit with my headphones on and think about everything they said. It's kind of bizarre. The Goodbye Girls is actually affecting the way people break up, like we're becoming a part of pop culture or something. Willa and I are pioneers.

I wonder if the guy who invented Facebook felt like this.

Garret's in line when I go up for my potato wedges. He smiles and nods. I pretend the napkins are stuck and focus all my attention on the dispenser. Out of the corner of my eye I see him carry his food back to his table and sit beside Trish. Like everything is normal.

I never noticed before, or watched any of the others. Do they all do that? Pretend right up until the last minute? Shouldn't they be dropping some hints? Giving the cold shoulder?

"Honey!"

In the same situation, would I be any different?

"Sweetie!"

Guess deep down we're all just gutless cowards.

"Miss!"

"Oh, sorry!" The lunch lady is glaring at me with her arms crossed. "Small wedges and a chocolate milk please," I say.

I'm careful to avoid Garret for the rest of the day. I don't even know if I have to. I'm just being pre-emptive. Willa's so convinced that he likes me...and she's really intuitive about these kinds of things....

I just don't want to deal with any of this right now. Not with Trish's impending basket delivery looming.

After school I walk home from the bus stop, dragging my feet the whole way.

The house is empty, but I hide out in my room anyway, continually checking the time and straining my ear for any Trish sounds.

Willa is delivering the basket by herself. She thought it would be best if I was home when she made the drop in case I ever needed an alibi. I wanted to ask, *Why would I need an alibi?* But something stopped me. I don't think I want to know the answer.

I look over at the clock again, then out the window. It's not dark yet. I still have time to get something to eat. On my way to the kitchen, I run into Trish coming in the door. She passes me in the hall without acknowledging my existence— pretty standard behaviour. She obviously doesn't suspect a thing.

I make myself some KD and take it to my room, pot and all. I sit at my desk, staring at it but not eating it. It's dark now. I wait. I feel like I'm in a horror movie.

The doorbell rings and I freeze, my hand still clutching the pot handle. My fear is that she'll yell at me to go answer the door. *Dammit.* I should have hidden out in the bathroom with the shower running. But then I hear Trish's footsteps as she passes by my bedroom and runs down the stairs.

I get up and press my ear to the door. My heartbeat vibrates loudly inside my head. I hold my breath, waiting for a scream, a slam, a foot kicking a wall. I actually picture her scooping up the basket and biffing it off the porch. But there's nothing, just silence that seems to last a long time. That's way worse.

She passes by my room again. I hear the crinkle of the basket's cellophane, then the click of her bedroom door. Should I go make sure she's okay? I tiptoe down to her door. My hand hovers over the knob. I can't be 100 percent sure, but I think I hear sniffling. I let my hand drop and go back to my room.

Once inside, I lean my back against the door. "None of this is my fault," I whisper.

CHAPTER 13

THERE'S NO SIGN OF TRISH WHEN I COME DOWN FOR breakfast.

"Apparently Trish is sick," Mom says before I have a chance to ask. "She's staying home."

I nod and watch her pour coffee into a Thermos.

"She was asleep when I got home last night," Mom continues. "Did you see her?"

I shake my head. "No. I was in my room practicing flute." That's a lie.

Mom stares at me like she's trying to read my mind. "Trish is never sick."

"Root Beer Mile," I say, looking away.

"Yeah...everyone gets sick at that, though. Doesn't really count."

She's sort of right. The Root Beer Mile is a long-standing tradition at the West. Run seven laps around the bus loop, stop after each lap and down two plastic cups of root beer. First one to finish without throwing up, wins. Pretty much everyone throws up.

Mom threads her arms into her coat. "So is there something going on I should know about?"

I shrug and reach for the cereal.

"I assume it's some kind of boy trouble?" Mom fishes.

I shrug again.

She gives up. "Well, if you manage to make eye contact with her, tell her I'll call later to check in."

"Okay."

"Have a good day, then." She collects her Thermos and heads out.

After she's gone I sit and listen for signs of movement from upstairs. Nothing. My phone chirps. It's a text from Willa: Hows trish?

Still don't know, I text back.

Willa texted a bunch of times last night to ask how it all went down. I kept replying, Don't know haven't seen her. I didn't tell her about hearing Trish crying. She's staying home sick, I text now. See u in English.

I leave my bowl of cereal on the table and tiptoe up the stairs and down the hall to Trish's room. Taking a breath, I rap lightly on the door. "Trish?"

No answer.

"You okay?"

I wait. No answer.

I reach for the knob and turn. It's locked.

"Trish?" I say it louder this time.

When she still doesn't answer, I knock again and rattle the knob.

"For Christ's sake!" Trish yells. "Could you please get a life and leave me alone?!"

Oddly, I find her insult comforting. She's definitely on track to making a full recovery. "Mom wanted me to tell you she's going to call you later." I wait a moment. She doesn't respond. *Marvel.* "You're welcome!" I shout.

Garret comes up behind me as I slam my locker door shut. "Trish here yet?" he asks.

"Nope." I start walking, my eyes glued to the floor. The grey-streaked tiles pass beneath my feet.

He doesn't say anything but continues along beside me.

"I think she has the flu," I add. I'm not sure why.

"I feel bad," he says, stopping outside the Drama room. "I wish I could go back and do it over."

My eyes stretch wide open as it hits me. He assumes that I know, that she told me, that she *confided* in me. He obviously knows nothing about our dynamic. At first I'm not sure how I should react. But then I decide to go with it. It's easier pretending that she told me than pretending I don't know.

"Do it over and not break up with her, you mean?"

"No." He shakes his head. "Still break up, just do it face to face."

"I'm not sure it would matter much," I say. Because I really didn't think that it would.

He leans a shoulder against the wall. "I could explain. You know, how I think she's awesome but we just didn't have much in common. That there's a guy out there who's a better match for her."

"Well, you sort of said that in your letter." *Shit.* I realize my mistake as soon as the words leaves my lips. My heart drops like a stone into my stomach. *Glunk.* I never read any of the letters, *ever.* But this time…I read Garret's. Just the first two paragraphs. It was by accident, really—like my eyes couldn't help it.

He doesn't seem to notice. He rakes a hand through his hair. "Yeah, but I could have said everything better. Maybe made it more heartfelt or something?"

It hits me again. He thinks Trish showed me the letter. And why wouldn't she? We're sisters. I'm so flooded with relief I'm about to pass out. All I can manage is a tiny shrug.

He looks directly at me. "Maybe I should have manned up and been honest about liking someone else."

I feel my breath get all clogged and wheezy. I cough to clear my throat. "Even if you had the chance for a do-over—even a hundred do-overs—I'd leave that part out every single time."

He laughs because he thinks I'm joking. He starts to say something, but the first bell rings and cuts him off. A stampede of students rushes up to the door and I let them herd me inside with them.

Trish stays in bed for another entire day.

On the third day she returns to school.

It may be my imagination, but it's almost like everyone parts and makes way for her when she walks down the hall. The whole thing kind of reminds me of a Bible story.

A group of Trish's minions spots her and hurries to her side, cooing and offering soothing hugs of support. I was half expecting them to hoist her on their shoulders and carry her off to wherever.

"See?" Willa says. "You never have to worry about her. She's like a cat. Always lands on her feet."

I nod. "I know."

"Come on." She drags me into a corner at the end of a row of lockers and starts rooting around in her knapsack.

While I wait for her to find whatever she's looking for, I notice Garret down by the gym door reading the bulletin board. Except for our band classes, I haven't spoken to him since our conversation outside the Drama room. I've been trying not to think about it or let myself read anything into his words, or what they may have meant.

"Let's get down to business," Willa says, flipping back the cover of a binder.

But I don't hear her because I'm still watching Garret. He looks up and our eyes meet. He smiles. I smile back. The same thing happened yesterday, except in reverse. He'd been looking at me. It's like we can feel each other's gaze….

"Lizzie!" Willa says sharply.

I jerk my head around. "Sorry."

She looks all stern and says, "So. Seems as we get closer to Christmas, things are ramping up."

I think about that. "Guess people don't want to get trapped into buying gifts for someone they're planning on breaking up with."

"Especially if they're going to be forking over dough for our services on top of that too." She runs her finger down the page. Her lips move as she counts, then she scrunches her eyebrows together. "It's gonna be tight."

My turn to scrunch my eyebrows together. "How tight?"

She makes a growling sound in her throat. "Dad's picking me up tomorrow. We're having dinner and then I get to stay overnight at his new apartment. Yippee," she adds sarcastically. "I've hardly seen him lately. He's feeling guilty and trying to suck up."

"Who knows, though? You might have fun."

"Doubt it. Like, what are we going to talk about? How he's too busy living like a teenager and reinventing himself to spend any time with his kids?"

I tilt my head. "That sounds like something your mom might say."

She looks at me for a second. "You're right. She did." Her eyes get a bit watery. "I'm just so *mad* at him. He's making it really hard to stay on his side."

"Do you have to pick sides?"

She doesn't say anything.

"Well…try and keep an open mind. He probably needs time to adjust to all this. Just like you do."

"Yeah, maybe." She doesn't sound convinced. "I think I'm a little terrified he's going to sit me down and say he wants to start dating or something," she confesses.

At that moment a group of shrieking puck bunnies runs past us chasing a hockey player.

We watch them until they disappear down the hall.

"Because the last thing I need in my life is another brainless ditz," Willa says.

I pat her shoulder sympathetically. "Brainless ditzes are the worst."

She smirks and shuts the binder. "Anyhow, long story short, we have to go shopping today after school since the weekend's a writeoff. We have a bunch of baskets due next week."

"Oh no. I didn't bring any of our cash."

"No worries." Willa gets out her phone and starts texting. "I'll get Sean to pick us up. We can whip over to your place and get some on the way to the store."

Sean is waiting for us across the street from the school. We crawl in the back seat and Willa immediately starts barking orders.

"Yeah, yeah. First things first," he says. "I saw kids out selling Girl Guide cookies. Instead of food, I'll take a box of those."

"Cookies are still food, Sean," Willa says dryly.

He slams on the brakes, jolting us both forward. "Wanna walk?"

"God. Relax, would ya? I'll friggin' get you some!"

As we turn onto my street there's a crowd of young girls on the sidewalk lugging cardboard cartons.

"Remember when we used to do that?" Willa says.

I laugh. "It always seemed to be raining. Why did we do it in the rain?"

"We were kids. We didn't care. And it was a pretty easy gig. No one says no to Girl Guide cookies."

We slow down beside the girls and roll down the window. They back away from the car. I don't blame them. Sean's car is a 1999 Honda Civic, half black, half rust, with a trio of zombie bobbleheads suctioned to the front dashboard. There's a good chance they think we're drug dealers.

Willa waves a five dollar bill at them. The bravest one, probably the keener who wants high sales, edges toward the car, the carton of cookies banging against her knees.

An exchange of cookies for cash is made and we carry on our way.

I run inside my house. There's a box of Girl Guide cookies on our hall table. *No one says no to Girl Guide cookies.*

Willa put me in charge of holding the money. She says Sean seems to spend a lot of time prowling through the house looking for cash to "borrow." So all ours is in an envelope I keep stashed at the back of my sock drawer. I just have to hope Trish finds my neatly rolled and organized-by-colour socks as boring as she finds me. Taking out a wad of twenties, I grab my wallet off my desk, tuck in the bills, and race back down the stairs. Trish is lying on the sofa reading *Cosmo.* She doesn't say hi or bye. She doesn't even look up. *All's normal here.*

In the car I say to Willa, "Let me pay for the cookies, it's my turn."

"It's fine, I don't care," she dismisses.

"No, no. I have a five right here…" I poke through my wallet and find two tens folded up against all the twenties. "Or I thought I did." I hand her a ten. "This'll cover the cookies and a gas contribution."

She shrugs and jams the money into her coat pocket.

We make our usual stops and collect all the items on the list for the next set of baskets. At the last store there's so much stuff we can barely get it all to the car. I have about a dozen plastic bags hanging from my wrists. I can't feel my hands.

"We should have used a cart," Willa winces. "I think my back is broken."

"Carts are for rookies."

Sean sits in the front seat, earphones on, playing air guitar, as we unload everything into the trunk.

"Thanks for your help!" Willa says, smacking him in the back of the head as we get in.

"Hey!" he shouts, yanking out his headphones and spinning around. "I'm doing you a favour! If I helped you, it would be sexist. Like I was implying you weren't strong enough to do it yourself!"

"Ohhhh," Willa drawls. "Thank you *so* much. I didn't realize you were so into women's equality." They glare at each other in the rear-view mirror while exchanging obscenities.

I stay out of it and massage my wrists, trying to restore circulation to my hands.

CHAPTER 14

WILLA POKES HER HEAD UP OVER THE RECYCLING bin then ducks back down beside me. "Are you sure the bell works?" she whispers.

"Pretty sure," I say.

We're hiding out in the side yard of our latest drop-off. It's freezing and I can feel the snow soaking through the knees of my jeans.

"Someone should have answered by now. It's taking too long." Willa sticks her head up again. "Shit. There's someone walking a dog. Once they pass, I'll run up and ring it again."

We lean against the recycling bin and wait it out.

"You never said anything about your visit with your dad," I say. "I kept waiting for you to bring it up but it's been a while, and I didn't want you to think I didn't care."

"Yeah. I've been trying not to think about it."

I expect her to elaborate, but she doesn't. "That bad?" I prod.

"Pretty much."

"Like how?"

"I dunno. Textbook guilt. Let me pick the restaurant, the movie, offered to take me shopping…I was actually sort of having a good time until he suggested we have a serious convo."

"Uh-oh."

"Yeah. I had the same reaction." She cups her mittened hands to her mouth and puffs. "He wanted to make sure I had no illusions about he and Mom getting back together. That divorce papers had been filed, and it's all for the best, but that it didn't change how he felt about me and Sean, blah, blah, blah…."

"Sorry, Willa."

"I mean, does he really want this? Like, how bad could it have been at home? It couldn't be worse than starting all over." She shakes her head. "Maybe he has to realize that himself."

"And maybe he will."

"Icing on the cake," she continues, "there was a ladies' scarf on the floor in his front hall closet."

"Ohhh." Her greatest fear.

"Yup," she nods. "And that's not all. I have the same one in a different colour."

"Okay. So?"

"It's from Forever 21!" she hisses.

I think about it for a second. Then I get it. "That doesn't mean she's young," I say. "She could be any age."

"Yeah, I know." She puts her face close to mine until we're nose to nose. "*We* shop there and we're only sixteen!"

I pull back. "Oh my god, Willa. Your dad is *not* going out with someone *our* age!"

She holds up a hand. "Yeah, well, I didn't ask. I don't want to know." Then she shifts onto her knees, leans sideways, and peeks around the edge of the bin. "Okay. They're tying up a poop bag. They should be out of here any minute."

"Hey. Who's the basket for, anyway?" I'd had to work on a group project all last night, so Willa did up the baskets for this set of drops by herself. I hadn't bothered to look at tonight's list of who was breaking up with who. Sometimes it's less depressing not knowing.

"Claire McRae," Willa answers.

"Claire McRae," I repeat slowly. "Are you sure?"

"Yeah."

"From Bradley Parker?"

"Yeah."

I start shaking my head. "Bradley's locker is next to mine. He has his tongue stuck halfway down Claire's throat on a daily basis. I have to manually move them out of the way so I can open my locker door. They don't even notice."

"He could just be playing the role…like, up to the bitter end."

"No. No way."

Willa takes another peek up over the bin. "The coast is clear. I'll try the bell again."

I grab her arm. "You're not listening to me. They've been going out for two and a half years. Bradley is *not* breaking up with Claire."

She tugs her arm away. "Well, he placed the order," she argues.

"Trust me," I say. "It's got to be some kind of mistake. God. Just this afternoon he was telling Gary Nickelson how he's making a promposal video for Claire."

She slumps down beside me. "Really? Are you absolutely sure?"

"Yeah. They were standing at his locker. I heard the whole thing."

Willa bites her bottom lip. "Maybe I should have been more suspicious of the letter."

"The letter? Never mind." There's no time to wait for an answer. I take another quick look then make a break for Claire's front door. I grab the basket, run back, and skid into the bins as if I'm sliding into home base. A moment later, a minivan turns onto the street, then pulls into Claire's driveway. "We got lucky," I pant.

She helps me up. "Let's get back to the car before we freeze to death."

We dart across the neighbour's yard and tumble into Sean's back seat.

"Jesus. What took you guys so long?" he says. "Did you stay for dinner or something?"

"Shut up, Sean!" Willa shouts. "You'll survive five minutes without food." She stretches her arm toward the front, reaching for the heat control.

He swats her hand away. "Don't touch the knobs!"

"But we're *frozen!*"

They keep arguing back and forth until I interrupt. "Pleeease, Sean," I say in my most syrupy-sweet voice.

"See, Willa?" Sean says. "It's called *manners*." And he cranks on the heater.

The warmth seeps into my skin, making my cheeks tingle. As I begin to thaw, my brain starts computing. "What were you saying about the letter?"

"Bradley requested that we enclose a *sealed* letter from him in the basket, not like the ones everyone else emails and we print off." She pulls the basket up onto her lap and starts rummaging. "He said that since they'd gone out for so long, he had some personal things he wanted to say, wanted to let her down easy, stuff like that. I didn't see a problem with it." She holds up the letter. "We should open it."

I shake my head. "No, not yet. What if I'm wrong—though there's no way I am—and Bradley really *does* want to break up?"

She sticks out her lower lip and stares down at the letter. "Yeah...I guess we should wait."

"Because theoretically, Bradley knows it's going down tonight, and obviously it didn't. If he actually ordered this basket, we should hear from him tomorrow wanting to know what the hell happened, right?"

"That makes sense." She reluctantly sticks the letter back in the basket. "Maybe by some miracle I didn't empty my folders and I still have his email. We could see if something's there—though I'm not sure what."

Back at Willa's, we tear up to her room. She fires up her laptop before she even takes off her jacket.

"It's gone," she says, and slams her laptop shut. "Damn me and my efficiency."

It was our strictest rule. Delete every email immediately, empty all sent and deleted folders, clear any browsing history, leave no trail. I can't really get mad at her for following protocol.

"Do you remember anything about his email?" I ask. "Anything that seemed weird, or maybe didn't sound like him?"

"Well, like what? I don't know him. So I don't know if it sounded like him or not."

"And the email address? You're sure it was his?"

"Yeah...it was his Halifax West account. I remember seeing the 'ednet,' but I don't remember the actual address." Willa taps her fingernails on the lid of her laptop. "Really. It was just a standard request."

"Except for the letter," I add, and I mull this over for a minute. "So how'd you even get it?"

"The letter? It was in an envelope inside the envelope with his payment."

"Hmmm." I nod. "It's actually a good idea. I'm surprised more people don't do it. It's way more private."

"People are too lazy. It's an extra step. Plus, our email letters *are* private." She looks at me sideways. "We don't read them."

"No," I say quickly. "Of course not."

I think about all the letters I've printed off. All the letters I glanced at, but truly didn't read, Garret's letter that I *did* read, part of, sort of. I wonder if Willa has read any. And is she right? Are people really that lazy, that they'd rather take the chance someone reads their emailed letter than print it off themselves and put it in an envelope?

I sink down onto her bed. "Well, we can't open the letter or do anything until we hear from Bradley."

"Or don't hear," Willa points out. "You know, now that I think about it, he did order the cheapest package. Kind of weird if they've been going out for over two years."

"Yeah," I say. "That is totally weird."

CHAPTER 15

SATURDAY GOES BY WITH NO WORD FROM BRADLEY. I'm stuck home working on a PowerPoint presentation, but Willa has been texting me every hour to say, Still nothin. I tell her to hold off. I can't help second-guessing myself. Like, I'm no relationship expert. Who knows what's going on in Bradley's head? But if Bradley didn't order the basket, who did?

Hot chocolate in hand, PJs and fuzzy slippers on, I hunker down for a super fun night of finishing my presentation, doing a Science lab, and getting a start on my English essay. I swear the teachers hold some kind of secret meeting where they decide to make everything due at the same time just to stick it to us.

I'm home alone, so at least the house is quiet and I'll get stuff done. Trish is at some party—like she usually is on Saturday nights—and even Mom is out. She still won't tell us anything. I guess I understand. It must be all kind of unfamiliar, kind of weird for her. I peel a giant flake of nail polish off my thumbnail. It's sort of depressing when your forty-five-year-old mom's social life is more exciting than your own.

My phone chirps. Another text from Willa. Let's open the letter we can reseal no one will know.

I read her text over a couple times. It *is* tempting. No it won't kill us to wait a bit longer.

Easy for you to say.

I try to concentrate on my homework, but I keep going back to wondering—if Bradley didn't place the order, who did? So I try to think about it logically. Could be someone playing a joke on Claire, or Bradley, or…could someone be trying to break them up? Yeah. It could be any of those. I turn the sound off on my phone and shove it under the sofa cushion.

My bazillion assignments are too overwhelming. I can't decide where to start. I end up channel surfing instead. No wonder people go out on Saturday nights; there's nothing on TV. Maybe I need some sustenance to get the ideas flowing. I make up a batch of chocolate chip cookie dough. Only about half makes it to a cookie sheet. The other half I eat raw out of the bowl.

I'm on the couch licking the last remnants off the spatula when I feel a vibration under my butt. My phone. I reach between the cushions and pull it out, expecting to see another text from Willa. But it's not Willa. It's Garret. My heart starts banging against my rib cage. I read his text.

Hey Lizzie at Simon Clarks party not far from your place you should come over.

I stare at it for what seems like ages, to give myself a chance to process the words. The time on the top corner of my phone says 10:37. My curfew is midnight. There's a brief moment when I actually consider it. There's no one here to say I can't. Then reality sinks in. It'll take me an hour to decide what to wear…plus, it's mostly grade twelves, and I'm 99 percent sure that's the same party Trish is at. I'd show up and she'd be all like, what the hell are you doing here? And I'd be all like, Garret invited me, and yeah…things would not end well.

With the rubber spatula hanging out of my mouth, I text back, Thanks for the invite would really like to but totally up to my eyeballs with class presentation stuff. Party responsibly :)

He replies a few minutes later. Ha ha 2 late good luck see you in school.

A bit dazed from what just happened, I go out to the kitchen to clean up my mess. *Did Garret just kind of ask me out?* I can't believe it. It's like a dream come true. Then reality sinks in for a second time and the dream dies right here, because Trish would have a cow. No joke. She would have an actual cow.

I debate texting Willa and telling her what happened. But something stops me. Like maybe I want to keep it to myself and savour it for a while.

Phase two in the big push to finish my assignments involves falling asleep in front of the TV. Sometime later a noise wakes me up. I blink a few times till my eyes can focus. *SNL*'s Weekend Update is just finishing up, so I know it's late. I hear the noise again. It's coming from the front door. I'm about to go investigate when Trish stumbles into the hallway.

"Man," she whispers super loud. "My key wouldn't fit in the lock." Her words run together to make one.

I roll my eyes. *The door's not even locked.*

"Is Mom asleep? I know I'm late." The more she tries to be quiet, the louder she gets. "She'll kill me."

"Mom's still out."

Trish's jaw drops. "Whaaat?!" The look on her face is as if she just won the lottery. She points to the stairs. "I'm just gonna go to bed before she gets home."

"Good idea," I say.

When she gets to the top landing I hear her say, "Way to go, Mom!"

The responsibility of staying up till Mom gets safely home is left to me. Talk about a role reversal. She waltzes in almost an hour later.

"Lizzie!" She's surprised to see me. "Why aren't you in bed?"

"I wanted to wait for you. Make sure you made it home okay."

She smiles. "Well, thanks for that, *Mom*."

I notice her cheeks are flushed and her hair's a little messy. It occurs to me that she and mystery man may have just been making out in the car or something. *Ew.*

"You must have had a good date, huh?" I say, trying to fish a little. "It being so late and everything."

"Oh, I don't know if I'd call it a date, really." She reaches for a coat hanger, avoiding eye contact.

"What would you call it, then?"

She doesn't answer and makes a big production about straightening out her coat and hanging it in the closet.

"Okay. So…like…what's he like?" I ask, not ready to give up. "When do we get to meet him?"

Mom turns and raises her eyebrows. "When's the last time you or Trish told me anything about *your* relationships?"

"Mom." I fold my arms. "This is totally different."

She smiles again, then glances up the staircase. "Did Trish get in on time? She's been pushing her luck lately."

"Um. Yeah. I think so," I say. "I was sort of asleep on the couch."

She looks at me like she's trying to figure out if I'm lying. "Get to bed, missy." She stands to the side and waits for me to go up the stairs. I do. She follows right behind.

A knock on my bedroom door wakes me up the next morning. Mom sticks her head in. "Willa's here. She says you're expecting her."

I rub my eyes, prop myself up on an elbow, and reach for my phone. It's 10:02 A.M. I flop back on my bed. *The letter.*

Mom sighs. "Well?"

"Just send her up."

"Yes, Your Highness."

My eyes won't stay open. My brain barely let me sleep. I couldn't stop thinking about Garret and our textual exchange. Is it possible he really does *like* me? Like, *like* like me?

I feel Willa throw herself across the bottom of my bed, crushing my feet. "Wakey, wakey. It's been thirty-six hours and no word from Bradley."

"Can I at least brush my teeth?"

"No."

"*Fine.*" I sit up and lean against the headboard. "Did you bring it?"

She looks at me like I'm crazy. "Of course I did." She whips the letter out of her jacket and waves it in my face.

I take it from her. There's nothing written anywhere on the envelope. I flip it over to check out the seal. "I might be able to peel it open. Or we could try steaming it."

"No time." Willa snatches it back and tears the end off.

I throw my hands in the air. "So much for *that* plan."

"We can just put it in a new envelope if we have to." She pulls out a folded piece of paper and opens it. I can't explain it, but subconsciously I brace myself. *Please just let it be a normal breakup letter from Bradley....*

The paper is blank, but sitting inside the fold is a photograph. I slide over closer so I can see. We each hold an edge.

Willa leans her head in toward mine. "Is that...Claire?"

"Taking a hit from a bong?"

We look at each other with giant eyes. "Shit," we say in unison.

"Isn't her dad a minister?" I say.

"And isn't she always trying to organize anti-drug rallies at school and stuff like that?" Willa says.

I nod. "She was in Trish's Drama class. She did a whole monologue on 'Just say no to drugs.'"

We take another look at the picture.

"Which leaves the question, where is Bradley?"

"I don't see him," Willa says. "That's a West party. Recent. Like this year. I recognize some of the grade tens."

"He must not be there," I say.

At that moment my bedroom door bursts open. "Do you have the Advil in here?" It's Trish. Willa shoves the photo under the duvet. We freeze like statues and try not to look guilty.

Trish narrows her eyes and stares at us. "What's up, nerds? Trouble down in Nerdville?"

"Nope," I say. "No trouble. No Advil."

Willa pinches me, then says, "Hey Trish. What do you know about Bradley Parker and Claire McRae?"

She leans against the door frame. "You mean, Bradlaire?"

"Yeah. I guess," Willa says.

"Well, I know some people find Claire a little heavy-handed, you know, with all the anti-drug stuff, but she's just doin' her thing. She's a total sweetheart. And the best thing that ever happened to Brad."

"Why?" I ask.

"He used to be a real partier, bad stoner, a complete mess."

Willa and I look at each other, and say, "Really?"

"Yeah," Trish says. "Claire really straightened him out. I'm partnered with him for our big Business Tech project. He's been great, a completely new person."

"Wow," Willa says.

"They sound like a match made in heaven," I say.

Trish narrows her eyes again. "Why all the questions?"

"Oh, um." Willa's eyes flit around the room. "We were just trying to figure out couples who were going to the prom. Like already formed couples. Right, Lizzie?"

"Yeah, like…" I try to think of something to add. "Is it better to go with someone you like romantically, or just a friend?"

"I think a friend," Willa says, a fake serious look on her face.

"Me too," I say, wearing the same fake look.

Trish slowly starts to close the door. "You guys are friggin' weirdos."

When we hear it click shut, Willa turns to me. "We're *good*."

"Thank you Drama 10," I say.

"So did Bradley send the basket or not?" Willa asks.

"No. We would have heard from him by now, wanting to know why it wasn't delivered."

"Maybe he assumes it was."

Doubt starts to niggle into my brain. "I suppose he might not expect to hear from Claire, not after the picture and everything. He'd know she'd be totally pissed."

"And mortified."

"Yeah. Mortified and horrified."

Willa jumps up. "It's not too late. We can still deliver the basket."

"No, no," I say, shaking my head really fast. "Who are we kidding? There's no way Claire would go all this time without getting in touch with Bradley—she doesn't know about the basket or the picture. Bradley should be chewing us out, saying, 'Why is she still talking to me like everything's normal?' So yeah, something's not right."

Willa huffs and jams her fists into her hips.

"Let's just wait until school tomorrow. As soon as we see Claire and Bradley, we'll be able to tell what's going on."

"And how's that, do you figure?"

"Don't worry. We just will." I try to sound convincing.

She doesn't look convinced.

CHAPTER 16

THERE'S A SPIDER ON WILLA'S CEILING. WE'VE BEEN lying on her bed, flat on our backs, watching it for almost an hour, and it hasn't moved an inch.

"Do you think it's dead?" I ask.

"What, my soul?" Willa says flatly.

Monday went just as I expected: Bradley and Claire walking hand in hand down the hall, totally in love. Willa and I stalked them until they started making out outside the art room.

"I'm beginning to feel uncomfortable," I whispered.

"It's like a trainwreck," Willa said. "I can't look away."

"Okay, you two!" a voice bellowed.

We both jumped, guilty, because we assumed it was directed at us. Then we saw Mr. Adams striding toward

Claire and Bradley. "Break it up!" He stepped between them. "I'm sure you both have a class you need to get to."

They both nodded sheepishly and headed off in opposite directions.

We did the same, minus the sheepish nod.

So now we're back at Willa's, spider-watching and hard-core thinking.

"Well, I think we can safely assume Bradley doesn't want to break up with Claire," I say.

"Or if he does, he deserves an Oscar. Plus there's been no email from him asking what went wrong, and I didn't hear any gossip or anything like that. Everything seems like business as usual."

"I wish we could just ask Bradley. I mean, the order *did* come from his email address."

"We can't. Not without revealing we're The Goodbye Girls." She makes a popping sound with her lips. "If only I hadn't deleted all his info, I could *email* and ask him, like officially, from The Goodbye Girls."

"And there's no way to get his student email address?"

"Not that I know of…" Willa pauses. "How do you feel about breaking into the office?"

I can't tell if she's joking. "Yeah. We're not gonna do that, Willa."

The spider drops down a foot on an invisible thread. It inspires me to finally move. I roll over and pull the party photo of Claire out of my knapsack.

Willa rolls over too. "If someone wanted to screw with Claire, why not just mail her the picture?" she asks, resting her chin in her hands. "Why use The Goodbye Girls and waste all that money?"

Back and forth, I flick the corner of the photo with my fingernail. "Maybe whoever ordered the basket wanted

Claire to think it was from Bradley, and that he was really breaking up with her, because he found out—"

"That's she's a hypocrite and a liar?" Willa fills in.

I nod. "If I were Claire and I got that basket, got this picture, that's what I'd think."

"Yeah, but our baskets are supposed to, you know, be *nice*—take the edge off breaking up, lessen the pain. Sending that picture? It's more like an in-your-face, stick-it-to-ya thing."

I think about that. "If someone just wants to stick it to her, you're right. Why bother with the basket at all?"

Willa slides off the bed and begins pacing restlessly around the room. "Unless...the basket's part of it."

"Huh?"

"Think about it," she says. "What would have happened if we delivered the basket like we were supposed to?"

I tug on my lip. "That was probably Claire's dad in the minivan. He would have found the basket first."

"Some random basket on your porch with no name on it? Claire has two other sisters. I bet he would have opened that letter, even if it was just to see who it was for."

"He would have gone ballistic."

"Claire would be grounded for life, if not worse. And after it hit the fan, either Claire, maybe even Claire's dad, would confront Bradley. He'd deny having anything to do with it. Assuming they believe him, who would be next on everybody's hit list?"

"Us," I say. "The Goodbye Girls."

Willa nods. "They'd definitely be wanting to question us, all three of them. Because as far as they're concerned, we're the ones who sent the picture."

"I'm not sure, Willa. It sounds pretty elaborate. The planets would really have to be aligned."

"No." She shakes her head. "No, they wouldn't. That basket was going to be found by somebody, and that somebody would be hunting us down for answers."

"Wouldn't we just deny it, like Bradley? We *didn't* send it."

"But we delivered it. 'The Goodbye Girls' is right on the basket."

I squeeze my eyes shut. "We should really rethink those gift tags."

"It was supposed to be for advertising, not for linking us to a *crime*."

My eyes fly open. "A crime?"

"Well, the photo is from some West party. It's like a poster for illegal drug use and underage drinking."

I go back to staring at the picture and flicking the corner.

Willa plunks herself down beside me. "No matter how it would have gone down, they'd be looking to find out who is behind The Goodbye Girls."

"You really think someone wants to get *us* in trouble?"

Willa shrugs. "Not really. I mean, *no one knows we're The Goodbye Girls*." She exaggerates her words. "But I guess I don't want to rule it out as a possibility either. Stranger things have happened, you know?" She takes the picture and slips it into her side table drawer. "For now we should be on high alert, see what the next few days bring, if anything."

"Okay." I get up and reach for my jacket. "Maybe whoever's behind it will give up when they see that whatever it was didn't work. It's probably just someone wanting to screw with Claire or Bradley." I loop my knapsack over my shoulder. "I'm sure that's all it is." *I'm sure that's all it is.* Willa says saying something over and over doesn't make it true. I'm hoping she's wrong.

"Fingers crossed."

I happen to glance at the ceiling. The spider is nowhere to be seen.

The next morning when I go to drop my books off, Garret's leaning against my locker.

I try to casually smooth my hair. "Hey," I say.

"Hey." He moves aside so I can get to my lock.

"Did you want me?" I ask.

He smiles. "Now that's a loaded question."

I feel my cheeks burst into flames. "Ha, ha," I croak. It takes me two tries to get the right lock combination.

"Did you get your presentation done?"

"What?" I'm hiding myself behind the locker door until the redness in my face goes down a bit.

"You couldn't come to the party. You were working on a presentation."

"Oh right. How *was* the party?"

His head appears around the edge of the door. "The usual. Pretty dull."

"Sorry I missed it then," I joke.

He smiles again. Super white teeth. "Listen. They put out a new list of fundraising opportunities. Your name wasn't signed up for any. Thought maybe you hadn't seen it."

"Oh, uh…" I nervously scratch the back of my neck. I don't need to do any fundraising, but I realize that probably looks suspicious. He went out with Trish. He would know we don't have a ton of money. "Yeah, I haven't had a chance to check it out yet."

"Thought we could team up or something. I've sold the Christmas wreaths before. They're pretty easy. Everyone orders them."

"Okay." I can't think an excuse to get out of it, and I'm not sure I want to. Slamming my locker shut, I see Trish coming around the corner. I quickly step away and put some distance between me and Garret. "Sign me up," I blurt out as I start walking backward down the hall.

The rest of the morning drags on. In English, Willa sits beside me doodling all over her grammar worksheet. I can't concentrate either. And weirdly, not because of anything to do with Garret, but because I'm too busy staring at every person who comes into my peripheral vision, trying to assess their threat level. *Is it you? Or you? Are you out to get Brad? Or Claire? Or The Goodbye Girls? Did you get a basket? Are you super pissed? But we're just the messengers....*

After class we head to the cafeteria for lunch.

"I still haven't heard a thing," Willa says. "You?"

"Not a word."

She nods. "Good. Hopefully we won't."

"Should we maybe shut down for a while?" The whole Claire-Bradley mystery still had me feeling on edge. "Until we know for sure?"

"Yeah, we had that pre-Christmas rush, but it's slowing down now. We're almost at our goal and we still have about a month."

"Really?" The relief I feel isn't only because Willa agreed to the shutdown, but also because we're close to having enough money and being able to shut down *for good.* "Do we have any this week?"

"Just one."

I see the look on her face. "Oh, no. Amy?"

"Yup."

All along I've tried to keep disconnected from the couples breaking up, especially the dumpees. And truthfully, it hasn't been that hard. There are so many people at the West that I don't know, never even heard of, it's rare when there's someone I actually *do* know involved in the process. Even less so when it's a delivery from one of the other schools. But this time it's Amy Duggan. The order came in a while ago and I've been dreading it ever since. Willa and I have known Amy since grade one. We were in the same class every year until junior high. She's one of the nicest people I've ever met. Even Willa likes her, and Willa doesn't like *anyone*. Amy's shithead boyfriend, Trevor, is dumping her after two years.

"They had their first kiss at your grade eight Halloween party," I say.

"I remember. In the backyard. On the trampoline."

"This is going to be a tough one."

"No kidding."

"I hate Trevor Hayes."

"No kidding."

"Mom!" I check the time on my phone. The bus comes in ten minutes. "Have you seen my red scarf?"

Mom comes out into the hall. "The one with the white flowers?"

"Yeah. Do you know where it is?"

"Um…Trish needed something with school colours for some spirit thing." She cringes. "She left with it. I assumed she'd asked you."

"God, Mom! Why would you ever assume that?!"

She starts rifling through a basket. "Here. Wear something of hers." She pulls out a mint green scarf with pink dots. "This is her new one. If you try hard enough you can probably stain it at some point during the day."

I grab it and stuff it in my knapsack.

"And just a heads up. If I can manage to get the time off, I'm going to the Valley to visit Nanny and Grampy next weekend."

"Sure. Everything's okay with them, isn't it?" I ask.

"Yes, yes. Don't worry. I just haven't seen them for a while and I'm starting to feel guilty."

"Do you want me to go with you?"

"No. You stay and keep an eye on Trish."

"I can't promise she'll be alive when you get back," I say as I rush out the door.

"Have a good day, honey," I hear Mom call.

I'm out of my mind furious. I'm supposed to go wreath canvassing with Garret after school, and I *need* my favourite scarf. I planned my whole outfit around it. Trish's scarf doesn't match what I'm wearing at all.

Willa's already on the bus, saving me a seat.

"Hey," I say, flopping down beside her.

"Hey," she says back. "Looks like you had the same kind of morning as me."

I shrug. "Just Trish being a troll. What's your story?"

"Just Mom. Trying to pretend she doesn't want to put her fist through the wall."

"Oh?"

"Aunt Meredith said she saw Dad downtown last weekend, having dinner with some *young* woman."

"Don't you mean some *young* brainless ditz?" I try to lighten the mood.

She cracks a half smile. Her phone buzzes and she pulls it out of her pocket. Reading the screen she frowns. "Speak of the devil. Dad wants me to stay at his place this weekend. Sean too."

I watch her put the phone face down on her lap.

"I'm going to say no," she says. "It feels like I'd be setting some kind of precedent. You know, 'Every other weekend at Dad's.'" She turns and stares out the window. "You know, when he first moved out I thought he'd be all sad and lonely, that he'd change his mind and come home. But he's not sad *or* lonely. And I'm starting to think he's never coming home."

We both fall silent and listen to the drone of the bus, the yammering of the students around us. It's all the usual drivel, with some sporadic moments of kids singing along to bus radio.

I can't imagine what Willa is going through. My memories of my dad are hazy at best. What's it even like to have a dad in your life—even one who's making you miserable?

"Were your parents happy, Willa?" I ask.

She doesn't answer right away. "They fought a lot. Yelled a lot. Well, it was Mom doing the yelling. Dad never said anything." She sighs. "Maybe that's worse. Not saying anything."

"It could turn out they're happier apart. You know, eventually."

She just shrugs.

"They say there's nothing worse than being in an unhappy marriage."

"They?" She spins around. "Who's *they*?"

I immediately regret bringing it up. "I dunno," I mutter. "I think I heard it on *Dr. Phil* or something."

"Because I can think of a lot of things worse than being in an unhappy marriage. Say, like having cancer, being murdered, burning to death in a house fire."

"Willa…" I attempt to reason with her. "That's really morbid, and I don't think that's what—"

"And what's his *girlfriend* going to do all weekend if we're there?" she says. "I suppose she could come over and we could read *Teen Vogue* together."

I open my mouth to say something like maybe the woman's just a friend, but she cuts me off again. "I don't want to talk about it anymore." And she goes back to staring out the window.

The school day passes quietly. It's been a while, and there's still no word or even a whisper about anything to do with Claire and Bradley.

"No news is good news," Willa says as we head to the front entrance. She holds the door open for me.

"Oh." I hadn't had the chance to tell her about the fundraising wreaths. "I'm not going straight home, I'm meeting Garret to go sell Christmas wreaths."

She raises her eyebrows. *"Really."*

I explain to her how Garret noticed I hadn't signed up for any fundraising activities and so not to arouse suspicion, I agreed to sell wreaths with him.

"That's actually a clever move." Then she gives me a sly smile. "Though I'm sure it will be a huge hardship for you." She elbows me in the side. "Text me later with all the deets."

Garret waves to me from the school driveway. Deciding to give his neighbourhood the first shot, we walk to his house.

The conversation comes easily. We talk about teachers, the New York trip, his plans for university. Usually I feel awkward and can't think of anything to say around people I don't know well, especially boys, but there's something about Garret. It's like I've known him forever. I'm actually pretty chatty, and… funny. He laughs at everything I say. I'm on fire.

We manage to get about twenty people signed up for wreaths, then hit Tim's for a well-deserved reward. Garret orders a coffee for himself and a hot chocolate for me. We both have a sour cream glazed donut. He pays for it all and points to a table.

I do a quick head check before I sit. *Phew!* Don't seem to be any of Trish's friends here.

"That wasn't so bad, was it?" he says, peeling the lid off his coffee.

"No. Not at all."

"It's better when you have someone to do it with. Makes the time go faster. So yeah, thanks for coming."

Willa's words echo in my head: *I'm sure it will be a huge hardship for you.* I smile and blow on my hot chocolate.

He goes on to tell me how he's counting down the days till the new *Star Wars* movie opens and how he bought tickets for himself and his dad a month ago but hasn't told anyone because all his friends would think he's a nerd.

"Nothing wrong with being a nerd," I say.

He nods. "Or maybe I just need new friends."

It sort of feels like a date, but it's only six o'clock...so I guess it's not.

Later that night when I'm doing my homework, Willa starts with the texts. The short version of my wreath expedition with Garret doesn't cut it, so I have to *start at the beginning and leave nothing out.* It's almost midnight when I finally crawl into bed.

"I think the Claire-Bradley thing was fluke," Willa says, passing me a stack of paper. We're helping Mr. Fraser organize the new sheet music into piles before band class. "I think whoever was trying to cause shit got the message and gave up."

I don't say anything. I still didn't feel 100 percent convinced.

"You should come for supper," Willa says.

"Sure."

"Then we can drop off Amy's basket."

"Oh, right. Amy." I'd pushed that to the back of my head.

"Mom will be working and we've got a ton of Thai left-overs—a break from tacos. And I know Thai is your favourite," she sings. "Might help take the edge off ruining Amy's life."

"I wish. I know it's Trevor who's *really* breaking up with her, but I still feel sort of guilty."

"I know. But it's just business."

"I suppose so…wait. Your mom's gone back to work?"

"Yup." She smiles. "Started yesterday. She's redoing the menu. She's wearing real people clothes and everything. No pyjamas."

"That's great, Willa."

"I think the girlfriend sighting lit a fire under her or something. She says it's time to channel all her emotions into being creative."

"So something good came out of it."

"I'm guessing the result is going to be a lot of cup-cakes with black icing and names like Murder, Mutilation, Dismemberment, Strangulation, and Death. All by Chocolate."

I laugh. I can't help it.

At Willa's I text Mom to tell her where I am and that I'm staying for dinner. We go to the kitchen and start pull-ing takeout boxes from the fridge. Everything's fine until she opens one of the containers. "Sean!" She wails like a wounded animal and slams it on the counter. Then she shoves me out of the way as she storms into the family room.

I flick through the recipe calendar hanging next to where my shoulder smacked into the wall and wait for them to fight it out over whatever.

"There were five spring rolls left, Sean!" I hear Willa shout. "Why is there only one in the box?!"

"Because I ate the other four," Sean replies.

"They weren't all for you, you know!"

"Then put your name on them next time."

"You're a pig, Sean! A shitty little pig!"

Willa blows back into the kitchen, face bright red. "He's a shitty little pig," she announces.

"Yeah, I heard." I pick through the cartons on the counter. "Don't sweat it, Willa. There's tons of food here."

After she does some deep breathing exercises and calms down, we sit at the table and stuff our faces with pad Thai, ginger beef, shrimp curry, and jasmine rice. We split the one remaining spring roll.

"So how's Trish doing?" Willa asks.

"Good, I guess. It's not like she'd confide in me or anything."

"I heard Jordan Short's going to ask her to prom."

"Really?"

"Not positive, but I was behind two of his friends in the bus-pass line. I think that's what they said."

"Wow. He was one of our first customers."

"Victims," she points out.

I think back to how awful I had felt. Knowing what was coming for Jordan, and him all oblivious. "Dumpee," I correct.

"But look, he survived. And maybe he'll be happier with Trish," she says, choking back a laugh. "Though I can't imagine." She starts stacking the empty takeout boxes. "Okay, we can't put this off forever. Let's take care of Amy."

Willa goes to sweet talk Sean into taking us on our delivery run. Of course he refuses. Can't really blame him.

"You're up," Willa says after her failure. "He likes you."

I go into the family room. "Sean, pleeease," I beg. "It's our last job for a while, promise."

He's playing on the PlayStation and doesn't take his eyes of the TV. "She treats me like shit, then expects me to drive her around town like a friggin' servant."

It's hard to argue that point. "That's just her way, Sean. She does it out of love."

He burst out laughing. "That's so funny I'll do it. For you."

"Thanks, Sean."

"With a few conditions."

I cross my arms. "Shoot."

"She has to apologize, you guys have to start giving me more gas money, and I want a Christmas bonus."

"Sure." It all sounded reasonable to me. Willa will just have to suck it up.

After Willa's extremely dramatic yet *un*-heartfelt apology, we climb into Sean's car and head for Amy's.

Something dawns on me. "We know this is legit, right?"

"Yeah, already thought of that," Willa says. "This order came in way back but was delayed because Amy's been off for two weeks. Jaw surgery."

"How nice for Trevor to wait till she recovered."

She nods. "Plus, I saw Trevor twice today and both times he was hangin' around with Sarah White…so yeah, I think it's legit."

CHAPTER 17

THE HOUSE IS DARK. THE DRIVEWAY IS EMPTY. THE only light comes from the faint glow of the street lamp on the corner.

We're crouched down behind the woodpile.

"I'll do it," I say, flipping up my hood and tying it snug under my chin.

Willa moves out to the end of the pile for a better view of Amy's front door. "Okay. I got your back."

I grip the handle of the basket and make my way up the yard, keeping to the edge, so that I'm under the trees. When I'm even with the porch, I cross the lawn. I've only taken about two steps when lights flash on, illuminating the entire yard. A dog starts barking from inside the house.

Shit! Motion lights! I clutch the basket to my chest, momentarily paralyzed. *Drop and run!* I place the basket on the grass and race toward the woodpile. I'm almost halfway there when I realize the dog's still barking and no one has come to the door yet. *There can't be anyone home.* I stop and go back for the basket, but not before seeing Willa waving her arms frantically like she's having some kind of spasm. As I set the basket on the porch, the dog starts barking again and the front door swings open. Instinctively I look up. It's Amy. She's in a robe and has a towel on her head. *Shit!* I turn and tear down the steps but somehow miss the bottom one and end up sprawled flat on the gravel walkway.

"Oh my god, are you okay?" I hear Amy ask.

Keeping my face hidden, I jump to my feet and sprint back to the woodpile.

"Hey! Wait!" Amy calls.

Shit, shit, shit. I don't stop running except to grab the shoulder of Willa's jacket and drag her along behind me.

Back at Sean's car, we lean against the trunk until we can catch our breath.

Shit, shit, shit. I repeat it over and over again.

"I saw the shadow of a person go by the window. I tried to warn you," Willa squeaks out between gasps. "Did she see you?"

I flick my hood off, push my sweaty hair from my forehead. "Yeah. I'm pretty sure she did."

"Dammit," Willa says, then, "Wait. Turn around."

I do.

She pulls my hood back up, tucks my hair in and ties the strings tightly. "Was this how you had it?"

"Yup."

She grips the fur trim on both sides of my head and pulls my face in close to hers. She studies me for a few seconds then shakes her head. "Even if she *did* see you, I don't think she'd know it was you."

I frown. "Really?"

"No offence, but without seeing your hair, there's nothing remarkable, nothing that stands out about your face." She takes a step back, looks me up and down. "You could be anybody. And everyone and their dog has a coat like that."

I lightly touch my fingers to my generic cheek, glance down at my generic black puffer jacket from Joe Fresh. "Gee, thanks."

"I *said,* no offence."

Hoping Willa's right but not wanting to risk it, the next morning I opt for extra layers of sweaters and leave my jacket hanging in the closet.

By lunchtime it's apparent it was all for nothing. Amy's not in school.

In the cafeteria, Willa sets her tray down beside mine and puts two of her garlic cheese fingers on my plate. "Save me from myself."

"Thanks."

"Have you seen Amy this morning? She wasn't in Science."

"I'm pretty sure she's not here."

She squints at me. "You don't look so hot. You okay?"

"You're just full of compliments lately, aren't you?" I'm still stinging over her comment about how unremarkable I am.

"I criticize because I love," she says. "You look a little pasty and tired, that's all."

I drive my fingers into my eye sockets. "I am."

"Well, if it makes you feel any better, I put up a notice on the website that we aren't taking any more orders for now, that we are experiencing technical difficulties," she says out of the corner of her mouth.

Yay! my brain screams.

"I figured we should probs lay low until we figure this out. I can tell you don't agree with me that it was just a fluke."

"Thanks, Willa. And yeah, it does make me feel better."

"No prob. But it's only for a little while," she adds.

There's not a lot of time left until Christmas vacation—a little over two weeks. I know Willa's trying to get in a few more deliveries before the new year, just for spending money. I made my second-last payment for the trip a while ago. The final one's due the last day of school before break. That's all I care about. I don't need spending money. What I really want is to just stop now.

Trish's friends Madison and Olivia walk by our table on their way to the grade twelve table. It seems like they slow down, and Madison...looks at me. Then they keep going.

I start fanning myself with a scribbler as droplets of sweat erupt along my hairline. "Did you see that?"

Willa bites the end off a garlic cheese finger. "No. What?"

"Madison. She looked at me, for like a long time."

She pours me a puddle of what the caf tries to pass off as donair sauce. "You're just being paranoid."

Am I? Am I just being paranoid?

Between living in fear that one of Trish's evil minions spotted me and Garret at Tim's and being terrified of coming face to face with Amy and seeing that flicker of recognition in her eyes, I'm seriously considering joining the witness protection program.

And how can I forget about the possibility that a random someone's out to get me, or Willa, or both of us, or The Goodbye Girls? *Jesus!*

I slide my chair out from the table. "I'm going to the library to read."

"Are you sure you're okay?" Willa asks.

"Yeah. Just having a claustrophobic moment or something."

"Okay, I'll come meet you after I brush my teeth." She puffs out a mouthful of air. "Garlic breath."

I make my way to the library, and who's standing right outside the door talking to the gym teacher? Garret, of course. Who else would it be when I'm literally looking like a decomposing corpse?

I tiptoe backward and hide in a corner at the end of a row of lockers.

Willa shows up and wedges herself in the corner with me. "Who we hiding from?"

"Garret."

She nods. "Got it." She squishes in tighter.

I love how no further explanation is needed.

The next week passes with no incidents. Everything seems normal with Trish and her friends—they're all carrying on in their usual bitchy way. There's no new developments with Claire and Bradley—they appear to be nauseatingly in love—so maybe whoever was behind that basket *has* accepted defeat. But for now all our business is suspended, which means I get a break. I swear the stress is starting to make my hair fall out. I keep pulling gobs of it out of my brush.

The only glitch is that Amy hasn't returned to school yet. Willa said she heard someone say she had an infection, something to do with her jaw surgery. So I can't be sure if she knows it was me who was in her yard that night or not.

"In the highly unlikely event that she *can* ID you," Willa says, brushing some nail polish on her thumb, "it's Amy. She'd probably apologize because her front steps were responsible for your fall. Also, I can't see her having any interest in blowing our cover. She's way too nice."

We're hanging out at the makeup counter at Shoppers Drug Mart, trying all the samples and making the cosmetician cranky. We walked down after school. Our P.O. box rental fee is due.

I don't respond. Instead I spray some of Taylor Swift's perfume on my wrist and sniff.

"So…how are things going with Garret?" Willa opens another colour of nail polish and paints her other thumb.

"There are no *things* going with Garret. We're just friends."

"Oh, Lizzie. Please help me sell wreaths," she says in a supposed Garret-like voice. "Though I'm a six-foot-tall football player, I'm just not capable of doing it by myself."

"That's the worst imitation I've ever heard." I spray a blast of Chanel N°5 into the air. "This is Mom's perfume." Then I walk through the mist. "This is how she puts it on."

Willa nods, looking impressed. "Fancy."

"Are you sure I can't help you ladies?" the cranky cosmetician asks tightly.

"No, we're good, thanks," Willa says, cracking open another bottle of nail polish.

The cranky cosmetician sucks in her cheeks, resulting in some bright coral fish lips, and returns to the far end of the counter.

I check the time on my phone. "We should go, shouldn't we? Isn't your dad picking you up at five?" Willa finally agreed to spend a weekend with her dad, and she has mentioned numerous times that she's looking forward to it like she looks forward to going to the dentist.

"Yeah, yeah," she says. "Soon."

After Willa has every fingernail painted a different colour and the cranky cosmetician is on the verge of a nervous breakdown, we finally leave and start for home.

"You never did answer my question about Garret," Willa says.

"Oh. Well. There's nothing to say. We're going out again. To sell wreaths," I clarify.

"But you like him."

I shrug. "What's not to like? It would never be worth it, though. You know. *Trish.*"

As we cut across the parking lot, we pass by McDonald's. Through the window I can see Trish standing at the head of a table, hands on her hips, holding court, lording over her subjects.

Willa follows my gaze. "*Might* be worth it."

"Okay, so I plan on being home by suppertime Sunday," Mom says, reaching for her overnight bag. "Look after your sister."

"Will do," I say.

"And the Mitchells know I'm away. Mrs. Mitchell will be watching this house like a hawk, so no funny business."

"Mom," I say. "Look who you're talking to."

She smiles. "You're right. Wrong kid." Turning at the door, she says, "Try and have a little fun, okay? Maybe you and Trish could have a movie weekend or something."

I choke back a laugh. "Yeah. Sure, Mom."

I watch her pull out of the driveway.

And so begins my watch. Trish will be home soon. My only fear is that she'll have all her idiot friends with her. I sit in the living room, right in front of the window so I can see the street. I have this insane need to protect my turf. *The cafeteria ladies aren't the only ones who need riot shields.*

Trish shows up about an hour later alone, carrying grocery bags. I follow her into the kitchen, surprised when I don't hear the clanking of bottles as she puts the bags on the counter. I had assumed it was all liquor.

"What's up?" I ask.

She seems distracted, searching through one of the bags. "Prom committee stuff."

I raise my eyebrows. "You're on the prom committee?"

She looks up, a big scowl on her face. "*Yes.*"

"Sor-ree," I mutter. Trish doesn't exactly seem like the prom committee type. I can't help feel a bit surprised.

"Anyhow, a bunch of us are going to Madison's to make grab bags and stuff for the coffee house."

"So…not here?"

"Oh my god." She throws back her head. "You're not going to cry about being left home alone, are you?"

"No," I say, all defensive. "I'm home alone all the time."

"Yeah, no kidding," she smirks.

Bitch. "I just thought, you know, with Mom gone…."

"What? That I'd throw some wild party? Yeah right. You'd rat me out in a nanosecond, and then there's Mrs. *Snitchell* next door. I wouldn't stand a chance."

It's weird. I was so prepared to do battle, I almost feel disappointed that there isn't going to be one.

"Plus, I don't have time," Trish says, whipping open cupboard doors and dumping random stuff into bags. "This is our biggest fundraiser of the year. We've got way too much shit to do."

Wow. Trish, a doer. Who knew?

"Okay," she says, taking a last look around the kitchen. "I'm outta here." She scoops up her grocery bags. "Later, loser."

For a long time I stand in the kitchen staring at the empty doorway, wishing that just once I could think of some vicious and witty comeback for Trish. I never can, though. That's more Willa's thing. But man oh man...just *once* would be nice.

My phone chirps. It's Garret.

Park lanes showing spaceballs tomorrow nite 1 nite only do you wanna go?

I hesitate, but only long enough to replay Trish's "later, loser" in my head.

Sure, I text back.

CHAPTER 18

THIS MORNING COMES WAY TOO SOON. I STAYED awake most of the night having mental arguments about how insane it was to say yes to Garret.

I pull on my housecoat and step out into the hall. The house feels empty. Weird. On weekends Trish rarely comes out of her lair before noon. Maybe she never came home. I stick my head in her room. Her bed's messy and there're clothes all over the floor, though that doesn't really tell me anything.

Over my Eggos I text Willa and ask her how it's going at her dad's.

She texts back: K I guess. I picture her making a face and shrugging her shoulders.

Then I text her about Garret asking me to a movie.
WHAT!!!???
I know right?
What movie?
Spaceballs
????
I think it's a spoof of starwars
Not very romantic...
I'd rather funny
Ya right.

There's a pause, then another text.

Gotta go dad making us go out for brunch check in later.

I sit for a minute, phone still in my hand, and think about what to do next. Then it dawns on me. I actually have a date with Garret. *Tonight.* I dump my dishes in the sink and tear upstairs. I only have about eight hours to figure out what to wear and get ready.

Quickly I flick through every hanger in my closet. I go so fast I don't think I even look at anything. I don't have to, because I know nothing's going to work. Next I dig through my chest of drawers. It only takes a few minutes before my room is an exact replica of Trish's.

I wade through the mess on my floor and head for Trish's closet. *Yuck. She really does have horrible taste.* I'm about to leave her room when I see her latest issue of *Cosmo* on her desk. I scoop it up, along with her giant makeup bag, which is really more like a makeup...suitcase.

Emma, Emma, where are you, Emma? I thumb through Trish's magazine looking for Emma Stone's latest Revlon ad. I've seen it a bunch of times and love her makeup in it. *Bingo.* I rip out the page and stick it on my mirror, then I line up all of Trish's tubes, bottles, brushes, pencils, compacts, and lipsticks. My eyes sweep back and forth between Emma and the array of makeup. *Yeah, I totally got this.*

I allot an hour for shower and hair straightening, an hour for makeup, a half hour to figure out what to wear, a half hour for getting dressed, and an hour to do my nails and toenails. It's December, so I don't know why I'm doing my toenails, but like, what if I twist my ankle and I have to take my boot off? Garret would tell me to take my sock off to check the swelling…I can't risk it. My toes better look good.

The countdown begins. I keep listening for Trish, hoping she stays away. She'd take one look at me, know something was up, and start machine-gunning questions.

Garret texts to say he'll pick me up at nine thirty.

Must be a late movie. Ok, I text back.

Don't eat we can grab a burger at Darrell's then head over to theatre

Grab a burger? Before the movie? I have no choice. I have to ask. What time's movie?

1130

Eleven thirty? Uh-oh. I'm supposed to be home by midnight.

He must clue in when I don't respond. Sorry should have mentioned that. Problem?

I tap a freshly painted fingernail against the side of my phone. It'll put me at least an hour and a half past curfew. Tap, tap, tap. I could call Mom and ask, explain the situation…but if the planets align, Mom won't even find out. Trish will *probably* be MIA, and if she does come home to sleep, it's likely it'll be past her curfew and I'll still make it back before her. No, it's fine, I text.

It's around a quarter to nine when I finish my transformation. I look in the mirror, tuck my hair behind my ears. *I'm as good as I'm gonna get.*

I text Garret and ask him to pick me up around the corner. I tell him I have to feed my neighbour's cat. Though Trish still hasn't come home, I can't take the chance that she'll show up, or pop in to get something, between now and nine thirty. All she'd have to do is peek out the window and she'd recognize his car. Then—well, I shudder to think.

I pick a house with an empty driveway and stand on their lawn trying to look casual. Garret arrives a few minutes later and honks. I wave and jump into the car.

"How's the cat?" Garret asks.

"Haven't starved it yet."

"Speaking of starved, I hope you are. Have you been to Darrell's?"

I shake my head.

"Then you *have* to try the peanut butter burger. It'll change your life."

I make a face. "Really?"

"Trust me. It will *literally* change your life."

I do have the peanut butter burger, and it does literally change my life. "I'll never go back to a plain ol' burger again," I say, wiping melted peanut butter off my chin.

He grins and passes me another napkin. "Told ya."

We finish up and sit for a minute, both with a hand on our stomachs, stuffed, then pry ourselves out of the booth and make our way to the theatre.

While waiting in the ticket line, I do a quick scan of the lobby to make sure there's no one I recognize. It's clear. Not surprising. *Isn't it almost bedtime?*

I was right about the movie. It's a spoof of *Star Wars*. It was funny, in an eighties kind of way. I laughed a lot. Garret laughed way more than just a lot. One time he laughed so hard, I actually thought he was choking. He recovered just as I was about to flag down an usher.

"Do you want water or something?" I whisper.

"No," he croaks. Then he laces his fingers through mine. "I'm good."

I basically lose the thread of the movie after that, concentrating only on the feel of his hand, warm, around mine.

When the movie ends and the lights come on, we leave the theatre and walk along Spring Garden Road. It's decorated for Christmas—wreaths on the street lamps, twinkling lights and ornaments in all the shop windows. It's pretty, and *sort of* romantic. Willa will be happy. We grab a coffee and a hot chocolate at Tim's and head back to the car. I don't look at my watch because I don't want to know how late it is, I'm having too much fun.

"I hope you didn't find it over-the-top cheesy," he says. "It's probably not for everyone."

"No, no, it was…good."

He raises his eyebrows.

I laugh. "No, really, it was."

He gives me a serious look. "Because you know they don't make them like that anymore."

"There might be a reason for that," I say out of the corner of my mouth.

He nudges me with his shoulder. "Ha, ha."

I nudge him back.

The drive home is quick. It's after one thirty and there are hardly any cars on the roads. As we get closer to my house, I realize I can't let him drop me off at home, for the same reason I couldn't let him pick me up there.

I reach out and put my hand on his arm. "Can you pull over here?"

He gives me a puzzled look. "Okay." He parks against the curb. "What's up?"

"Nothing. I want to walk the rest of the way, that's all."

He laughs. "I'm not going to let you walk a block by yourself this late at night."

"It's fine, really. I just want some fresh air."

He laughs again. "No way."

I might as well tell the truth. "Okay, look," I sigh. "One, I'm way past my curfew, and two…" I'm actually sort of surprised he hasn't figured this out. "I don't think it would be a good idea if Trish saw you dropping me off."

"Oh. Well, one, you should've told me about your curfew, and two," he says, giving me a sheepish look, "I get it. Though in my defence, I think she's moved on. She has a prom date already, and it's only December."

"Yeah, I know. I just don't want to make any waves. And anyway, if everything goes as planned, I'm going to sneak in and no one will be the wiser."

"Okay, I'll walk you from here."

"Nope." I shake my head. "That would be even worse. Trish seeing us walking down the street together…" *Gawd.*

"Then I'm getting a bit closer so I can watch until you're in your house."

I agree if only to end it, because the whole debate thing is making me even later.

He inches up a few more houses and stops. As I'm putting my gloves on, I notice a group of shadowy figures walking up my street. They're tall. All of Trish's friends are tall. Then I see a red hoodie. I lean toward the window, trying to see if WEST is printed across the front.

"Kill your lights," I hiss.

My eyes follow the shadowy group until they stop in front of a house and go up the front walk. It's the Cooper kids and their friends. They're all in university, so no threat there. I let out a breath I didn't realize I was holding.

"You okay?" he asks.

"Yup," I nod.

"Well, it was a fun night, huh?"

I smile. "It was."

He leans over to kiss me, but a taxi turns the corner and its headlights shine right into our car. I cover my face with my hands and throw myself forward, like I'm trying to hide my identity. Why? I don't know. But I feel his chin bump my ear on the way down.

He jerks back. "Are you *sure* you're okay?" he asks slowly. "Because there's no one out there."

"I know, sorry." I'm so jumpy. If I stay here one more minute, he's going to think I'm a raving lunatic. More than he already does.

I push the door open and scramble out. "Sorry," I say again. "I gotta go. I had a great time, thanks!" And that's it. I leave him sitting there, probably thinking I'm off to rendez-vous with the spaceship that'll return me to my home planet.

The house is dark. Could Trish be asleep? Or more likely, she's taking advantage of the fact that Mom's away.

On the off chance Trish is in fact home, I unlock and open the front door as quietly as I can. As soon as I do, the living room light flicks on. She's sitting on the sofa. Lying in wait. *Shit.*

"Well, well, well. Look who decided to come home," she says.

"Yes." I smile tightly. "You got me. I'm late. Why are you even home, anyway?"

She doesn't answer my question. "No note, no phone call, no nothin'."

I don't say anything.

"I was really worried," she says, her voice full of fake concern. "You *never* leave the house. God. I thought you'd been kidnapped."

"And what? You were waiting up for the ransom call?"

She smirks. "So where were you?"

I'd planned for this moment, just in case, as I'd walked from Garret's car. "I went to a party."

"With who?"

"Willa."

"Whose party?"

"Ava Clark's. She's in band. Grade ten. So you don't know her." I don't really know her either, but I follow her on Instagram and I know for a fact she was having a party tonight. If Trish does any detective work, I'm covered.

She squints her eyes. "Your makeup looks good."

I squint back at her. She says stuff like this sometimes. I think it's to throw me off balance. Is she sincere? Sarcastic? Passive-aggressive? I can never tell. "Thanks," I say.

"Don't worry." She pats my shoulder on her way to the stairs. "Your secret's safe with me."

I lay in bed wide awake for a long time going over every minute of the date. I think I was pretty on point till that last bit in the car. Then I start thinking about Trish and how she said she'd keep my secret. I almost believe her, basically because I'm betting she's smart enough to realize I have way more on her than she could ever have on me.

At least I *hope* she's smart enough.

Mom's not home ten minutes before I'm summoned to the kitchen and charged with my crime. Surprise, surprise. Guess Trish isn't that smart after all.

"I can't believe you stayed out until almost two, Lizzie," Mom says, slamming a pot onto the stove. "You're the last person I'd expect that from. Trish, sure, but not you."

"Hey!" Trish says looking all offended.

"I'm really sorry, Mom. But I wasn't drinking or anything. We just lost track of time."

"Who lost track of time?" she demands. "Where were you? Who were you with?"

"With Willa. And some other band people. It was a birthday party." Saying it's a birthday party somehow makes it sound more innocent. I feel terrible lying to Mom, but I have no choice. Trish is standing right there. I have to stick to the story I told her.

"Willa was with you?" Mom asks.

"Yup."

She turns her back to me and starts opening a can of something. I wait. "We'll talk about this later," she says stiffly. "You can…go clean the bathroom."

I frown. "But I just clean—"

"Do it again," she says, almost shouting.

As I brush past Trish, I say, "Thanks a *lot*."

"Hey, missy!" Mom calls after me.

I stop.

"Trish didn't say a word, by the way. It was Mrs. Mitchell. She couldn't tell me faster enough. I wasn't even out of the car."

I wince. *Damn you, Mrs. Snitchell.*

Do u wanna come over? Willa texts.

Can't think I'm in trouble, I text back.

But I want to hear about the date.

I told u everything. And I had, first thing this morning.

And ur sure u didn't kiss?

Um pretty sure. What did u do last nite? I try to change the subject.

Boston Pizza and new James Bond movie.

I heard it was good.

Boston Pizza was.

Haha.

I could come to u say we doing homework.

Maybe. I'll text u back later.

I set my phone down then pick it back up again. I tap on Garret's last message. I text, Thanks for last nite I'm still full, and press send.

Instantly he replies. Next time we should go to Darrell's on a Monday 2 for 1.

He wants there to be a next time. I text him back a happy face.

I drag myself down the hall and knock on Trish's door.

No answer. I go in anyway. She's lying on her bed scrolling through her phone.

"I'm sorry that I thought you told on me," I say.

She ignores me.

I sigh and start to back out of her room.

"It's okay," she says. "I'd probably think it was me too."

"Well, still, I'm sorry."

"You know, it's kind of nice to see you be a rebel, break the rules. You're always such a princess."

"Gee, thanks."

"And no offence, it's also nice to see *you* get in trouble for once." She goes back to scrolling through her phone. "Mom's really mad at you. It's the highlight of my weekend."

Supper's a silent affair except for the constant vibrating hum of my phone in my back pocket. There's no way I'm taking it out, though. Mom would lose it. I can tell she's in a mega bad mood. I feel the vibration again. I cough to cover it up.

I keep waiting for her to hand down my sentence, but she doesn't, and I'm not about to bring it up.

Excusing myself to get the ketchup, I practically crawl inside the fridge to check my messages. They're all from Willa. I don't take the time to read them, but judging by the amount and frequency, it's safe to assume something's up.

"Um…do you think Willa could come over? We have to finish an English assignment." I'm getting way too comfortable with the lies.

Mom lets her fork clatter down onto her plate and looks at me for what seems like a solid minute. "Maybe you and Willa should have worked on it last night instead of going to a party."

I just stand beside the table and don't respond. Part of me wants to wait till Trish is out of earshot so I can tell Mom what I *really* did last night. Maybe she'd be more understanding? But the other part of me is still not so sure how she'd feel about me going out with Trish's ex-boyfriend, who broke her heart, and then lying about it. Don't know if it's worth the risk. Finally I say, "You're right. I'm sorry."

"You've got an hour," Mom says. "Not a minute longer."

"Thanks." I quickly clear the table and load the dishwasher, all without being asked. Out in the hall I text Willa to come. It's as if she's here before I press send. If I didn't know better I'd think she was hovering out on the sidewalk this whole time.

She sees my surprised face. "Sean drove me," she explains, kicking off her boots and racing me upstairs. "Have you been on Facebook?" she asks over her shoulder.

"No."

She shoves aside the binder and textbook on my desk and sets up her laptop. Plunking herself on the chair, she opens up her Facebook page. "Okay. So listen to this post from Becky Duncan: 'The Goodbye Girls has gone to the dark side.'"

"What does *that* mean?"

"It took me a while to figure it out," Willa says. "But from what I can tell by the comments, *someone* is pretending to be The Goodbye Girls."

"*What?*" I go over and squeeze myself onto the edge of the chair beside her. "Why?"

"And they delivered a basket to Allan," she continues.

"Allan, our tuba player?"

She nods. "Yeah. Last night."

"But why Allan? And why do they think it's The Goodbye Girls?"

"There was a tag on the basket, just like ours, *saying* it's from The Goodbye Girls."

"But he doesn't even have a girlfriend. So who would be dumping him?"

She raises her eyebrows. "You haven't even heard the worst of it."

My stomach flip-flops. "There's more?"

"Oh yeah. Seems the basket contained a few…unusual items. The most notable being a Ken doll with its head ripped off, and a container of brownies—you're not going to believe this—iced with Ex-Lax."

"*Ex-Lax?*"

"You know…the laxative?"

"Yeah," I sigh. "I know what it is, it's just…*what*?"

"Apparently we're all just hearing about it now because he's been *glued* to the toilet for the past fifteen hours."

"Oh god." I scratch my forehead. "But wouldn't he wonder about the basket? Think it was kind of sketchy? Like, who eats random brownies from a basket that has a headless Ken doll in it?"

We look at each other. "Allan," we both say. Then we sit quietly, almost like a moment of silence for poor Allan.

"How would you even ice brownies with Ex-Lax?" Willa asks.

"There's the pill kind, but there's also a version of it that looks like little squares of chocolate. Tastes pretty much like chocolate too."

"How do you know so much about it?"

"My grandmother always has it in the house."

She scrunches up her nose. "And you would be able to make icing with it?"

I shrug. "You'd probably just have to melt it down, throw in some butter…icing sugar…."

"Yummy," she says making a face. Then she points at her laptop screen. "You should know, everyone thinks it's us, and we're getting some seriously bad press."

"But how? They must know it's not *really* us. We said that we weren't taking any orders right now. It's on our website."

"Yeah, well, they think we're lying. They think we're"— she pauses for air quotes—"'taking the business in a new direction.'"

I turn the laptop so I can see better. There, under the comments, it's just like Willa said, along with other comments such as, "How could they deliver that basket knowing what was inside?" and "What kind of person/people would do this?" and "They're so greedy they'll do anything for a price."

"They're right, except for the part about it being The Goodbye Girls." I turn the laptop back around so Willa can see. "Like, who *would* do something like this to Allan? He wouldn't hurt a flea."

"Which takes us back to the question: if this isn't about Allan, is this about us, or The Goodbye Girls?"

I think for a second. "Do you think it could be related to the Claire-Bradley thing? Could it be the same person who sent the party pic?"

"Maybe…but that basket was an actual order on the website. This is a…a…."

"A rogue basket?" I offer.

"Exactly." Willa clicks her laptop shut and shakes her head. "I seriously can't look at any more of those comments."

"So what now?"

"Well, I'll put a disclaimer on our website saying we had nothing to do with Allan's basket. With any luck, people will believe us." She doesn't sound too hopeful.

"Okay."

"Then, like before, I think we'll just have to wait it out, see what goes down at school. That's really the only way to gauge things."

I bob my head up and down in tiny nervous nods.

"Look," Willa says. "The masses can be all irate at The Goodbye Girls till the cows come home. But we're still safe. No one knows it's us." She threads her arms into her jacket. "So like, really, what's the worst that can happen?"

CHAPTER 19

"**S**HIT." WILLA STICKS HER ARM IN HER KNAPSACK and feels around. "Do you have an extra pen? I only have pencils."

"Um...maybe." I unzip my own knapsack.

"Got a French quiz, and that freakshow Madame la Croix will only let us use pen. I thought I had one."

All my pens and pencils usually roll around loose at the bottom so I start pulling things out and dumping them onto the bus seat between us. "Got one!" I raise it above my head as if it were the Olympic torch, but Willa doesn't respond. She's frowning at my giant pile of crap. "I know," I say. "Secretly I'm a hoarder."

She looks up at me then back down at my pile. "No, this." She pulls Trish's scarf out from under my makeup bag and my key chain full of mini highlighters.

"Oh. That's Trish's. Forgot I had it. A while ago Mom told me to take it and spill some food on it."

Willa's frown deepens.

"Long story," I say.

She rubs the material between her fingers. "This is the one I have but in a different colour."

Nodding, I scoop up my stuff and start throwing it back into my bag.

"It's the one from my dad's apartment," Willa says still holding the scarf. "The one that was on the floor in his closet."

I stop what I'm doing to study the scarf hanging from her hand. "You mean it's *like* the one from your dad's apartment."

"Yeah, yeah," she says, rolling her eyes. "Okay…it's *like* the one from my dad's apartment."

I tilt my head. "Didn't you say it's from Forever 21?"

"Yeah."

"Well, there you have it. Half of Halifax probably has this scarf." I go back to re-packing my bag. "Not to mention Dartmouth," I add. "Because, like, what's the alternative? That Trish is having an affair with your dad?"

Willa laughs out loud. "He's not her type. He reads books and can talk in full sentences and stuff."

"Hey!" I give her a shove. "Then what are you saying about Garret?"

"I guess everyone's entitled to a lapse in judgement," she says dryly.

The bus jolts to a stop in front of the school.

I hear Willa take a deep breath. I do the same and comb my fingers through my hair. The scarf thing was a nice distraction from The Goodbye Girls situation, but now it's back to reality. Bracing for whatever awaits, we get in line and shuffle toward the bus door.

Inside, the first thing we see is Allan coming toward us. "Hey, Allan," I say hesitantly. I can't help feel a little guilty.

He smiles and waves as he passes by.

Willa and I look at each other and frown. Without a word, we turn and follow him. As we watch, it soon becomes apparent that he's okay with everything. People are slapping him on the back, high-fiving, tossing him rolls of toilet paper, and shouting things like, "Have you lost weight?" and "Hey, where's your throne?" and calling him "King." By mid-morning he's actually achieved a sort of celebrity status.

Bonus is, I don't once hear anyone mention The Goodbye Girls.

I'm suffering through double Math when Mr. Stevenson says, "Open your textbooks to page 115, and start on the first four questions. Please remember to show all your work."

The room immediately fills with the sounds of deep sighs and the rustling of paper. I notice Neil, who's in front of me, smells like he just crawled out of a bottle of Axe—every time he moves it seems to stir it all up. My eyes are practically watering and I can't concentrate on my work. Then a light bulb goes off in my head. I reach into my bag and pull out Trish's scarf. Looping it around my neck, I spread out some of the fabric so it covers my mouth and nose like an oxygen mask.

As I read the first math problem, I slowly breathe in and out through the scarf. At first I think it's not working because I can still smell something. But then I realize it's not the Axe, it's something different—nicer, more subtle. I know that smell. Chanel N°5. Mom's perfume.

I set down my pencil, tug the scarf off my face, and lean back in the chair. Why is Mom's perfume is on Trish's scarf?

Chanel isn't trashy enough for Trish. Then I remember that morning a while back, in the kitchen, and Trish saying, "Is that my scarf?" and Mom saying, "Yeah. I guess it is. You don't mind, do you? I think you actually still owe me for it."

My mouth suddenly goes dry. I keep running my tongue over my teeth, trying to make some moisture so I can swallow. But nothing's working. I feel like I'm going to gag.

I go up to Mr. Stevenson's desk and ask to be excused. He waves me away with his hand.

In the bathroom, I lean into the sink and talk to myself in the mirror. "Could this really be the scarf Willa saw in her dad's closet?" I loosen it from around my neck. It feels like it's choking me. "Mom and Willa's dad? Is it possible?" Not surprisingly, my reflection doesn't answer. I rinse my mouth out and splash some water on my face. I tell myself no way, what are the odds? It's too far-fetched. But the more I think about it, the more it doesn't seem that far-fetched. Actually, it seems *close*-fetched.

Shit, shit, shit.

Back at my desk, I try to concentrate on my math. It's no use. *Willa. What am I going to tell Willa?* I break out in a sweat just thinking about it. I tap the tip of my pencil on my paper over and over so loudly that Aidan, behind me, pokes my shoulder. "Sorry," I whisper.

I have to talk to Mom. I have to find out for sure.

I plan my escape. Lunch is next. I need to avoid Willa, so I text her that I'm staying for extra Math help, but I hide out in a practice booth in the band room—no one goes there. After lunch I have Science, then PAL. I can't get marked absent, or I could lose my exam exemption. After suffering through Science, watching the clock the whole time, I show up for the beginning of PAL, long enough for attendance to be taken, then I go up to Mr. Reynolds and tell him I'm having really bad period cramps. He shifts uncomfortably and nods without taking his eyes off his clipboard.

I scurry toward the exit. *Like taking candy from a baby.*

The halls are quiet and empty because classes are still in. I gather what I need from my locker and slip out the back door. I start speed-walking home, my mind racing just as fast as my legs. *It can't be true.* I pull an end of the scarf out from the top of my jacket, hold it to my nose, and inhale. *But it is.* Deep down inside, I know that it is.

I find Mom in the kitchen unpacking groceries. "Hey, honey. You're home early."

Without responding, I unwind the scarf from my neck and hold it up for her to see.

She glances up. "Oh. Did you manage to stain it up good?"

"No. No stains," I say flatly.

"Oh well, better luck next time," she says, stacking some cans in the cupboard. "How can we be out of cocoa?" she mutters to herself.

"Mom."

"Hmm?"

"Willa found a scarf exactly like this one at her dad's place."

I see her back straighten.

"I remember you borrowed this scarf from Trish," I say, and for what seems like the hundredth time, I bring it to my nose and sniff. "It has your perfume on it."

Red floods her cheeks as she turns and slowly sets down the box of cereal she's holding.

"It's too much of a coincidence," I continue. "It makes sense. That's why you wouldn't tell me anything about who you were seeing, why you said it's so complicated and all that. It's complicated, all right. You're sneaking around with my best friend's dad." I pause as something occurs to me. I smack my forehead with the palm of my hand. "That's why you were so mad at me for breaking curfew. You knew I was lying. You knew I wasn't with Willa. That she was with her dad. Because you guys talk."

I wait for her to say something. I thought at least she'd try to deny it, maybe even laugh and say I'm being ridiculous. Instead, she takes down a wine glass and places it on the counter. "There's an open bottle of wine in the fridge. Pass it to me, would you?"

I don't move.

She sighs and reaches around me to the fridge.

"Well? You're sneaking around with him, aren't you?" I say.

It takes her a while to answer, but she finally does. "I wouldn't exactly call it sneaking around."

"Keeping him a secret. Not telling us about him. That's sneaking around, Mom." Then something else occurs to me, and I suck in my breath. "You weren't seeing him when he was still with Willa's mom, were you?"

"Jesus, Lizzie. No." She yanks the cork out of the bottle. "What kind of person do you think I am?"

I toss the scarf on the table. "I'm not sure *what* kind of person you are."

She narrows her eyes. "I think I'll ignore that comment."

I watch her pour a glass of wine, pull out a chair, and sit at the table. I can't believe how calm she's acting, like there's nothing wrong. "How could you, Mom? How could you do this? What were you thinking?"

"Lizzie. I'm sorry you're upset, and I—"

"Not upset, Mom. Mad. Crazy mad."

"I know this might create a difficult situation, but I'm sure—"

"When were you going to tell me, huh?" I can't stop interrupting her. "After you guys run away and elope or something?"

"Now, that's hardly likely," she says.

"So what *was* the plan, Mom?" I say sharply. "Keep it a secret forever?"

"Of course we were going to tell you. And Willa. And Sean, and Trish. Everybody. We were just waiting...to see if there was something there, between us. I mean, it wasn't worth telling everyone if we didn't feel there was any future."

"Oh. My. God." I feel my eyes stretch wide. "You guys have a *future*?"

Mom takes a sip of wine and doesn't answer.

"Mom! You know what a shitty time Willa's had. You know that she wants her parents to get back together!"

"That's another reason we were waiting," Mom says. "We were hoping Marlene and Willa would start to adjust to the idea of Greg not coming back, and begin to move on."

"Mom! That's never going to happen."

"You said Marlene was doing better, that she was back to work. And that Willa wasn't fighting against spending time with her dad so much anymore."

"That doesn't mean she's doesn't want her family back."

Mom rubs her eyes. "I don't know what you want me to say, Lizzie."

"I want you to say you'll stop seeing him."

Again she stays quiet.

"*Mom!*" Frustrated, I throw my hands in the air. "Well, I'm going to tell Willa. Like, right now," I threaten.

She shakes her head. "Please don't do that, Lizzie. It's not our place—yours or mine—to tell Willa. It should be her father."

I fold my arms. "So *is* he?"

"Is he what? Going to tell her?"

"Yeah. *Obviously.*"

"Yes. Yes, of course he is."

"When?"

"I'm sure it will be soon."

"How soon?" I snap.

"I don't appreciate your tone, Lizzie," she says, lifting her chin. "I'm still your mother, and when you get right down to it, this really doesn't concern you."

"It does so concern me! You expect me to keep this huge secret from my best friend?"

"No," she says quietly, like she trying not to get angry. "I expect you to let Greg deal with it, and handle it the way he thinks is best."

My mouth hangs open. It's like she's turned into an alien pod person. "She already knows her dad's seeing someone," I say all snarky.

"Well." She takes a mouthful of wine. "Then is it really going to make that much of a difference that it's me?" Her face brightens. "Maybe it will make it easier."

"God no, Mom. It'll make it worse."

The brightness disappears. "Why?"

"I don't know." I feel like my head's about to explode. "It just *will.*"

"Lizzie. You're not making any sense."

I feel my eyes stretch open again, wider than before. "I can't believe this is happening!"

Mom reaches out to touch my arm, but I jerk away. She looks hurt. "I'm sorry you feel this way," she says. "But it's not like I woke up one morning and said, 'I think I'll make Lizzie miserable.'"

"You could have hooked up with *anyone*, Mom. But no. You hook up with the father of my best friend, my best friend who hopes every day that her parents will get back together."

Mom's lips straighten into a thin line. "One, I couldn't have, as you put it, 'hooked up with anyone.' Men aren't exactly pounding down the door of a forty-five-year-old woman with two kids."

I feel a stab of guilt deep in my chest. I know she's right. She hasn't been seriously involved with anyone in twelve years. Not since Dad died.

"And two," Mom goes on, "this wasn't planned. Sometimes things happen when you least expect it. He joined the gym, and we just began talking."

I flash to when Willa's dad was at her house fighting with her mom. The red gym bag by the door. You get it for free when you sign up. I should have recognized it.

"Of course we had met each other once or twice before, but that was about it." Mom shrugs. "We mostly talked about raising teenage girls, just chitchat, then we started to grab a coffee here and there…."

"Did he tell you about how wrecked Willa was, still is, about him leaving?"

A pained expression crosses her face. "Yes, he did. It tears him up."

Any bit of guilt I feel melts away. "But you still kept on seeing him, knowing how devastated his family was."

"Me seeing him wasn't going to change any of that. And really, in the beginning, I was just someone to listen to him, maybe even offer some advice."

"Maybe your advice should have been, 'Go back to your wife and kids.'" I can feel I'm getting close to crossing the line. But I don't care.

After a few seconds, she quietly says, "I don't think that's going to happen."

I shake my head over and over. This can't be real. "You know what Willa calls her dad's mystery woman? A brainless ditz!" *My mom's the brainless ditz.*

Mom's eyes narrow again. "I think you've said quite enough."

I start backing out of the kitchen. "You better tell your boyfriend to talk to his kid!"

"He's in Boston at a medical conference."

"Well, I'm not waiting for him to get back."

Mom stands up. "Lizzie!"

"I can't. Willa would do the same for me."

"Lizzie!" she calls out, but I'm already halfway up the stairs.

Grabbing my phone, I type out a text to Willa. Meet me at McDonalds. My thumb hovers over *Send*.

How am I going to tell you? How am I going to tell you my mom and your dad are a thing? A real thing? I stare at my phone. *And that your mom and dad probably aren't ever going to get back together. And maybe it's because of my mom.*

I hold down the backspace button until the message is deleted.

CHAPTER 20

I SPEND THE REST OF THE AFTERNOON IN MY ROOM sprawled on my bed, fuming to myself and rehearsing different ways I can break this news to Willa. But no matter how I spin it, it never ends well. I must doze off at some point because my stomach growling wakes me up. My room is dark. The clock radio glows 7:08 P.M.

Mom didn't call me for supper.

When I get to the kitchen, Mom and Trish are already finishing up their spaghetti. I don't say anything. Mom doesn't even look up. After piling some noodles onto a dish, I slump into my chair across from Trish.

There's zero conversation. I can feel Trish's eyes drilling into me.

She finally breaks the silence. "So, uh…" She waves her fork back and forth between Mom and I. "What's going on *here?*"

We both stay quiet.

"What?" Trish says. "Only get 99 percent on your math test, Lizzie?"

"Don't worry about it, Trish. It has nothing to do with you," Mom says.

"*That's* a first." She slides her chair back and carries her stuff to the sink. "I'll just leave you guys to it, then." She grins from ear to ear. "Play nice."

The silence hangs thick and heavy in the air, like smoke from a kitchen fire. I keep waiting for Mom to speak, mostly so I can give her the silent treatment, but she doesn't say a word.

"Aren't you going to apologize?" I blurt.

Mom looks up from her plate. "For *what?*"

"What do you think?"

"If you're talking about me seeing Greg," she says, throwing her napkin on the table, "I've already told you, I'm sorry you feel like I've put you in an awkward situation."

I push my noodles away. "Doesn't *sound* like you're sorry."

"I'm not apologizing for trying to grab a bit of happiness before I wind up in some nursing home."

"*Wow.*" I don't trust myself to say anything else. *When did she get so selfish?*

When she shows no reaction, I shove my chair away from the table and march out of the kitchen.

Trish is in the hall putting on her jacket. "You and Mom BFFs again?"

"No."

"Hmmm," she says, shoving her hair under her hat. "Don't sweat it. Whatever it is, I'm sure she'll come around."

I eye her suspiciously. *Is Trish actually being...nice?* I expected her to say something more like, "Wish I gave a shit." I shrug. "Yeah, maybe."

She smiles, which throws me off again, and hooks her knapsack over her shoulder.

For a second I toy with the idea of telling her what's going on, but I stop myself. *Let's not get carried away just because she had one human moment.* Plus she probably wouldn't even care. I watch her pull on a boot, then stop when her phone pings. She swears under her breath as she reads her screen and aggressively texts someone. She swears again and jams her foot in her other boot.

I frown. "Where are you going?"

"Oh, uh." Her phone pings again. "Prom committee stuff," she says distractedly as she types in another text.

After she leaves I glance back toward the kitchen, listening to the clatter of dishes. I usually load the dishwasher after supper. I stand there picking at a piece of peeling paint on the banister, then I head up the stairs to my room and stay there.

Now I'm going to miss *The Voice.*
Thanks, Mom. I hope you're happy.

Zombie. That's the word that comes to mind the next morning when I look in the mirror.

I'm not sure I even slept. I leave for school before anyone's up. For the entire walk I weigh the pros and cons of telling Willa about Mom and Greg. The pros are I think it's the right thing to do, and I owe it to her because she's my best friend. The cons are...well, the list goes on and on.

I'm at my locker when Willa texts me that she's home with a sore throat. Clutching my phone to my chest, I can't believe my luck. I know I'm just postponing the inevitable, but the coward in me will take what it can get.

At lunch, I sit in the far corner of the cafeteria directly behind a pillar and grind my chocolate chip cookie into dust. I just want the day to be over so I can go back home, hide in my room, and not talk to anyone.

"Hey!" Garret plunks down right across from me.

My eyes feel like they're about to pop out of my head. *God. I haven't thought of Garret once in the last twenty-four hours! Thanks again, Mom!* "Hey," I say in a strangled voice.

"Were you sick or something yesterday?" he asks spreading butter on his bagel. "I looked for you after school."

I nod. "I left early." I think of Willa. "Sore throat." Then I give myself a mental head slap. *Why did I say that? He won't want to kiss me with a sore throat. Whoa, get a grip, woman! It's lunchtime in the caf!* "I feel fine now, though."

"Seems like everyone's sick," Garret says. He goes on to tell me about how this morning someone in Calculus threw up in front of the teacher's desk and it caused a chain reaction, and two other students—

Thankfully, before he can offer up any more gory details, we're interrupted by some kind of commotion up by the cash. I can see Trish is there, big surprise, with a bunch of her minions. Whatever they're doing, it's really loud.

Garret jerks his head in their direction. "What do you think is going on there?"

I pretend like I'm intently studying the scene. "I can't tell if they're laughing or crying, so it could be one of two things. Either Harry Styles just got engaged, or someone scored a two-for-one coupon for a mani/pedi."

Laughing, he rips a chunk off his bagel. He slides an untouched piece toward me. "Want some?"

"No, thanks. I'm good."

He pulls back his piece of bagel. "So, um, we're having our year-end football banquet this Saturday. Do you think you might want to go?"

It takes a few seconds for the question to register. "With *you*?"

"No. With my cousin, Brian. Of course with me!"

I feel my cheeks burn. "Right, right. Don't mind me. It's, it's…the throat medication."

He laughs again. "Okay. So is that a yes?"

I fake a coughing fit to buy some time. We'll be together in public. What about Trish? I take a deep breath and smile. "Yes, it's a yes." *I'll figure something out.*

"Great." He slaps the table. "I'll let you know more when I get the details."

The bell rings and everyone starts getting up.

If only I could split myself in two. One of me could deal with all the crap so the other me could be full-on excited about Garret asking me to his banquet.

Not that I'm *not* excited. I'd just be so much more excited if I didn't have this stuff with The Goodbye Girls hanging over my head. Plus I'm stressed about the "Trish factor." Not to mention Willa and my mom, the homewrecker.

I text Willa and tell her about Garret. She texts me back right away. If her texts had a voice, my ears would be bleeding. I've never seen so many exclamation points.

Mom's at work when I get home, so my plan of hiding in my room and not talking to anyone is coming together perfectly. I don't even have my coat off when my phone chirps. It's a text from Willa. Get over here ASAP! At first I don't panic too much. She probably has a dress she wants to show me for the banquet. I text her, What? She doesn't reply. She *never* doesn't reply.

My stomach drops like a hundred-pound weight. *She knows about Mom and Greg. Somehow she knows.* Greg must have called her from Boston. How did she take it? Does she want to chew me out? Or maybe she doesn't know I know, and wants to break it to me herself. Will she believe me when I tell her I was about to do the same thing? Guess I won't know till I see her. I feel my body fill to the brim with dread, and re-button my jacket.

Willa's waiting for me at her front door and yanks me inside. "What were people saying at school?"

I'm confused. Why would people at school be talking about Mom and Greg? "About what?"

She gives me the same look that Trish always does, like I'm a complete moron. "The Goodbye Girls."

Thank god. "Um, nothing?"

Now *she* seems confused. "And nothing about Olivia?"

"Olivia?" It's like I've walked in halfway through a conversation.

"Olivia Munden," Willa says, all frustrated.

"Trish's friend?"

"Yes!"

"I didn't hear..." I scratch my forehead. "Wait. They were all together yapping about something at lunch, but...."

She grabs my arm and drags me upstairs. "Come on. We've got trouble. Trouble with a capital T."

"What do you mean?"

"There's been another rogue basket." She pushes me inside her bedroom and closes the door. "Someone claiming to be us again delivered a basket to Olivia."

"She goes out with Trent Butler, doesn't she?"

"Oh, it wasn't a *breakup* basket," Willa says, sitting down at her laptop. "Trust me. I wish it was."

Uh-oh. "What was it then?"

"It was a…chubby basket? A…I dunno." She taps the screen. "You tell me. She posted a pic on Facebook."

I lean over her shoulder. "It *does* look like one of ours." But only at first. From the photo I can make out a can of SlimFast, Weight Watchers pamphlets, a package of Dexatrim pills, some kind of diet bars….

I press my fingers to my temples. "Shit, shit, shit."

"Olivia is out of her mind. And from the comments, so is everybody else. Not feelin' any love for The Goodbye Girls at the moment."

"Don't read them to me." I feel the panic start to build in my chest. "I don't want to hear it."

"Shit." Willa scrolls down the screen. "She's saying it's a form of bullying."

"She's right." My breathing speeds up.

"Calm down," Willa says. "No one's looking at us. I just wish we could convince everyone it's not from The Goodbye Girls."

"Maybe put another disclaimer on the website?"

She nods. "And since Olivia and Trish are friends, maybe you could talk to Trish, fish around a bit."

"I'm not sure she'd tell me anything." My mind races. "I just don't understand. Who would do this? Who would deliver such a *mean* basket?"

"Everyone thinks *we* did." She turns to me and rolls her eyes. "It's the same type of comments as last time. Basically that we'll do anything for money."

"Why don't they believe our disclaimer?"

"Guess it's easier to believe it's us, than not."

A bead of sweat trickles down the small of my back. "We need to walk away from the business before someone connects us to it. Dissolve it. Kill it."

"We don't have to be *that* drastic," Willa says.

"Are you crazy? Why aren't you freaking out more?"

"Because I told you before, there's no way anyone can trace it back to us. Plus, we didn't *do* any of this!"

"Willa, please. There's enough money for the trip. It's not worth it."

"But we had tons of requests for bookings before all this started. It's still a viable business, beyond the trip stuff. We'll never have to work a part-time job again. I don't want to just give it all up. That means those idiots, whoever they are, win!"

"Nobody will want to book us. They hate us!"

"Right now they do, but hear me out. What if we find out who the hell's behind this and prove The Goodbye Girls is innocent? We can broadcast it to the world, and hang the guilty party in village square."

I have a moment in which I contemplate telling her about Mom and Greg just to distract her from all this. I open my mouth. "Willa…" But then I close it again. I just can't seem to form the words.

"Admit it. You must want to know who's trying to take us down." A smile slowly spreads across her face. "Let's get our Nancy Drew on."

CHAPTER 21

"I'M SERIOUS ABOUT CHANNELLING OUR INNER detectives," Willa says.

"Yeah." I nod. "I know."

"Okay. So what are our options?" she says all business-like. "Like, is someone out to get Claire and Bradley, Allan, and Olivia? Like, is someone pissed off at all of them?"

"Or…" I chew the inside of my cheek. "Are they pissed at The Goodbye Girls, or even at us, as in, you and me, and the others are just collateral damage?"

"One more time from the top," Willa sighs dramatically. "There's no way anyone knows it's us."

"Okay, okay." Wish I could feel as confident as she does. "So someone is totally pissed at The Goodbye Girls. We've obviously ruined a life or something along the way."

"I've no clue." She rests her chin in her hands. "That seems unlikely. I mean, to go to all this trouble?"

I review the dozens of breakups we've handled. I know people got hurt, but that's what happens in relationships, isn't it? Especially in high school. "I've no clue either," I say. "Because our business, it's just the vessel. Think of all the crap that goes on Facebook. I don't know of anyone trying to bring *it* down."

"Then, could it be us?" Willa asks. "But we barely associate with anyone." She starts shaking her head. "And no one knows it's us. No way."

I let my eyes flick around her room, racking my brains, trying to come up with something that makes sense. I zoom in on a family vacation photo on her dresser.

"There's *one* person who knows," I say.

Willa spins her chair around. "Who?"

"Sean. Sean knows."

"Sean," she repeats.

"I mean, he *must* know what we're doing. He takes us to get supplies, he drives us to all our deliveries, he's probably *heard* of The Goodbye Girls by now—he's still friends with some people in grade twelve. It wouldn't take much to put it together. It has to be him."

"I dunno. We're talkin' Sean here. I don't know if he'd necessarily put it together." She gets up to come stare at the same family photo. "Plus, what would be his motivation?"

"Well, don't take this the wrong way, but you kind of treat him like shit. Maybe he's had enough."

"But he likes you. He wouldn't sacrifice you to get to me. Not to mention, all this sabotage takes a lot of work. Sean is possibly the laziest person on the face of this planet."

"In every movie, it's the person closest to you, the one you least expect, who's guilty."

Willa twists up her mouth. "Sean may be a turd, but he's not the vindictive, vengeful type. He just wasn't born with those chromosomes."

I drag my hands through my hair. "You're probably right."

"Though…" Willa looks thoughtfully off into space. "I suppose we should leave no stone unturned."

"If only to eliminate him." I stand, straighten my sweater, and square my shoulders. "Let's do it."

We find Sean in the den on his PlayStation. "Sean!" Willa stands directly in front of him, blocking the TV.

He ignores her and leans sideways, his fingers frantically hitting buttons on the game controller.

"Sean!" Willa reaches behind her and turns off the TV.

"What the hell!?"

"I need to ask you something!"

"Jesus! Hurry up, then. I'm in the middle of an online game."

"Your loser friends can probably pull off the carjackings without you for *two* minutes."

Sean tosses the controller on the coffee table. "What do you want, Willa?"

She crosses her arms. "Are you trying to take down our business, or get me in shit?"

"Well, I'm *always* trying to get you into shit," he says, smiling. "But what business? What are you talking about?"

"Don't screw with me, Sean."

His eyebrows scrunch together until they become one long line. "You mean the basket stuff?"

"Yeah," she says impatiently. "The basket stuff. The Goodbye Girls. Our breakup business."

"Breakup business," he says slowly. "What's a breakup business?"

"We break up with people, *on behalf* of other people," I explain. "For money."

His face clears. "Wow."

Willa scrunches up her nose. "What did you *think* we were doing?"

"Dealing drugs," he says.

My jaw drops. "*What*?!"

He shrugs. "I figured the baskets were a cover, and you hid the drugs in the lining or something. I was actually impressed. It's kind of genius. I mean, who's going to suspect a couple nerdlingers like you two?"

"I can't believe you thought we were dealing drugs!" Willa exclaims.

He shrugs again. "Like I said, it's the perfect cover." He strokes his chin. "You know, if the business is going tits up anyway, would you mind if I took it over? Tweaked it a bit?"

Willa looks over at me with raised eyebrows. "I think we can safely cross him off our list." She reaches for my hand. "Come on." She marches out of the room dragging me behind her, but then she stops at the door and turns. "Did you tell anyone, Sean?"

"About what?" He flicks the TV back on.

She throws her head back. "About the baskets. Or our supposed drug operation."

"Nah." The sound of an explosion comes from the TV and he punches his knee with his fist. "None of my business."

"I think he's telling the truth," I say.

"Me too."

Back in her room we bellyflop onto her bed.

"So we're back to square one," I say.

"I think the key lies with Bradley. That's where it all started going sideways. His email—there's got to be something in that email."

I flip over onto my back. "Like what?" I ask.

"Guess we'll never know, since I deleted it."

There's a knock on the door. "Yo." The door opens before Willa has a chance to respond. It's Sean. "Dad just texted. He wants me to pick him up at the airport and he wants you to come."

"Why?" Willa whines.

"How would I know? I'm just tellin' you what he said. So don't go sayin' I didn't give you the message." He backs out and shuts the door.

A sharp pain starts to spread through my stomach. "Where's your dad?" I ask, playing dumb.

"At some convention thing."

"When's he coming back?"

"Late tomorrow night, I think."

My mind shuffles through all the possibilities. Does he know yet that I know? Is he going to tell them on the way home from the airport? Is that why he wants Willa to come? Or will he tell Marlene first? Maybe there's no point in me saying anything if he's going to tell them tomorrow. *Yeah.* I nod to myself. *I'll just stay out of it for now.*

Willa sits up on her elbow. "What are you doing?"

"What do you mean?"

"Your lips are moving."

"Oh. Um. Just…thinking of our next move."

"Which is?"

I'm on the spot and have nothing to offer. "Uh…uh… Bradley. I'm going to talk to Bradley."

Willa gives me a weird look. "And say *what?*"

"Well…we know somebody used his school email. You need a password. He must have *some* idea who would be able to access his account."

"But we've been through this. You can't ask him without spilling the beans. He'll want to know *why* you want to know."

I chew on a fingernail. "I'll come up with something," I say. *At least I hope so.*

"Okay. I'm going to...dammit!" she huffs. "I don't know *what* I'm going to do."

I put my hand on her shoulder, feeling guilty about what's coming her way. "Take a break. You've got a sore throat."

"Can't afford another sick day. Look what happened the one day I stayed home."

As I get ready to leave, I say, "You know, there's still going to be lots of talk about Olivia's basket tomorrow. You should do some hardcore eavesdropping. There might be a clue in there somewhere."

She gives me a salute. "I'm on it."

CHAPTER 22

THE NEXT DAY I'M LIKE A DOG HUNTING FOR HIS bone. Except in this case, the bone is Bradley. As I skulk around the halls, I can't help but catch snippets of conversation. Everyone's in a major flap over what was done to Olivia. They're calling it the fat-shaming basket, and they're also calling The Goodbye Girls complete pieces of shit. Which totally makes me crazy, because even if we *had* delivered the basket, which we *didn't*, don't they realize we'd only have been the messengers? *God. Everyone's so stupid!*

It's almost impossible, but I stay focused on my task of tracking down Bradley. It's not until the last block of the day that I overhear someone say he's home with mono. *Oh god. He'll be out forever!* I feel like slamming my head into the closest locker door.

When Willa joins me on the bus, she looks like she's just come off the battlefield.

"Whaddaya got?" I say.

"Not much." She rests her head back against the seat. "That's not completely true. I was listening to Olivia's friends outside the caf. They said she's calmed down a bit and feeling a little better," she whispers. "So at least that's something."

I rest my head back against the seat too, and close my eyes.

"Also." I feel her breath close to my ear. "FYI. I saw Olivia going into the guidance counsellor's office."

My eyes fly open. "What do you think that means?"

"Probably nothing good."

"Or maybe the guidance counsellor was the one who calmed her down."

"Maybe." She sits up. "What'd you find out?"

"Bradley's got mono."

"Crap," she says. "Hopefully it's a mild case." She touches her fingers to her neck. "I feel swollen. Can you get it without making out with someone?"

My phone chirps as I get off the bus. It's a text from Garret giving me the details about the football banquet. It's semi-formal, he'll pick me up Saturday at seven.

I press my hand against my stomach. I'm pretty sure I have an ulcer.

I have to tell Trish. The banquet's going to be full of people she knows. There's no way I can go in secret, word's going to get back to her faster than I can say "sistercide."

Trish's books and knapsack are in the hall when I get home. I find her in the kitchen, kettle in hand, filling a mug with steaming water.

I sit at the table wondering if that water is hot enough to leave scars.

She looks over her shoulder at me. "Want some tea?"

Great. She's being nice. That makes two days in a row. "No thanks. Uh, listen Trish. I need to talk to you about something."

"Oh yeah?" She squeezes out the tea bag.

"Yeah…uh…you know Garret?" I can hear my heart thumping in my ears.

She looks over her shoulder again and raises an eyebrow. "Yeah, I know Garret."

"Well." I swallow. "He needed someone to go to this year-end football banquet thing. And like we talk in band a lot and stuff, you know? And so he asked me to go, just because, like I said, he needed someone to take."

She shows no reaction and goes back to her tea bag.

"We're just going as friends," I add as I cross my fingers under the table. "But I don't want to upset you or make you mad, so if it bothers you at all, just say so, and I'll tell him I can't go."

She keeps her back to me, stirring her tea. She stirs and stirs for a long time before she taps the spoon against the mug and sets it on the counter. "It's fine," she finally says.

I'm afraid to respond, thinking it must be a trick.

She turns, leans against the counter, and blows on her mug. "Really. It's fine," she repeats.

"Are you sure?"

Her head bobs up and down.

"Because, like I said, if it bugs you or anything…and, like, I know how much you liked him and I don't want you to think I went after him. It just kind of, well we have stuff in common, and we were fundraising together." I decide to stop before I make it worse.

She rolls her eyes. "Don't worry. I don't think you set out to go *after him* or would do anything to hurt me *on purpose*." She takes a sip from her mug. "You're not the type."

"Good." I'm so relieved.

"That's more like something *I'd* do, right?" she laughs.

I'm not sure how to answer that, so I don't.

"Like, it's a good thing we weren't twins. I'd probably have absorbed you in the womb."

Ew. "W-what?"

"Oh, lighten up. God. Just kidding." She reaches into the cupboard for the Oreos. "I mean, I guess I can see it," she continues. "You're probably a better match for him than me." Then she smirks. "I'll deny that, though, if you ever ask me to repeat it."

I manage a smile. *Maybe she really is okay with it.*

"You should go. It'll be fun," she says. "I went last year with Jason King. It's semi-formal. The guys clean up real good." She smiles. It looks forced, but I appreciate the effort.

"Wow. Thanks, Trish. You're being so…nice." The phrase feels foreign on my tongue.

She gives me a sideways look. "We *are* sisters, after all. Can't do much about that. Trust me, I tried." She laughs again, then holds up a pinkie. "Sisters for life, right?" She stares at me, waiting for an answer.

A belt slowly tightens around my chest, making it hard to breathe, but I hook my pinkie around hers anyway.

After Trish leaves the kitchen, I sit there for a while. My heart rate finally slows and eventually goes back to normal. That wasn't so bad. It went way better than I thought it would. No cuts or bruises, and I still have all my limbs. I did it. I told Trish the truth and it went well! I'm actually feeling a little empowered, on a bit of a roll. Maybe if I do the right thing and tell Willa about my mom and her dad it will go the same way—maybe it won't be so bad either.

I drum my fingers on the table. If I'm going to do it, I should do it now, before her dad does. They're picking him up at the airport tonight, and if he's planning to tell them, there's a chance he might let it slip that I know. And shit. If Willa finds out that I already know and didn't tell her, she's going to be even madder about that than about my mom possibly destroying her family. I pull on my jacket and make a beeline for Willa's house. On the way I practice my opening line: "You know that scarf you found in your dad's closet? Funny story…."

I'll probably leave the "funny story" part out.

When Willa opens the door I notice her eyes are all red and swollen. "Are you crying?" I ask.

She sniffs and sweeps her fingers across her cheeks. "Come on in." Her voice sounds hoarse.

I follow her inside. "What's wrong?" I brace for the answer.

"It's the airport. I don't want to go. Like, why is he *summoning* both of us?" She sinks onto the couch. "I have such an ominous feeling about it. Every bone in my body is screaming that it's going to be bad."

Before I can say anything, her chin drops to her chest and her shoulders start to shake. "Mom told Aunt Meredith that deep down she thinks Dad's going to eventually come home. I heard her on the phone." She looks up at me. "I really, really want her to be right."

I sit next to her and wrap my arm around her.

"But what if she's wrong? What if tonight he's telling us that he's in love or something? Or that he's getting married?" Willa sobs. "What about my mom? What about me and Sean? What if this homewrecker has kids? He'll have a whole new family."

I can see the tears plopping on Willa's jeans, leaving dark stains. I sit there hugging her until her sobs subside a bit. Then I feel her tense up. "Doesn't she know my parents are still technically married? What kind of desperate loser starts dating a married man? She's either a gold digger or an idiot. Or both. God! I haven't even met her yet and I already *hate* her." Willa's voice is getting louder, trembling with rage and sadness.

There goes my plan. There's no way I can tell her, not right now anyway.

"You might be getting ahead of yourself," I say, fighting to keep my tone even and calm. "You don't know if he's going to say anything like that." *He'd* better *not say anything like that.*

"Yeah." Willa takes a deep breath and reaches for the box of Kleenex on the table. "Sorry."

I tighten my arm around her. "Don't be silly. Nothing to be sorry about." *Trust me. You're not the one who should be sorry.*

"It's just that I *know* my parents should get back together. They have to. They need a little time, that's all. Only I'm scared that someone's going to get in the way before they get a chance to work it out. I'm a total emotional basket case." She blows her nose. "Ha. Get it? I said *basket*."

"Ha." I try to smile.

She wads up her Kleenex. "I didn't even ask why you're here."

"Oh, I, uh." My eyes dart around the room. "Actually, I thought I might have left my Science binder here, but actually I think it might actually be in my locker." *Shut up! Stop saying* actually!

"You sure? I can check upstairs."

"I'm sure." I stand. "I should run back to the school…"

She nods and we both walk to the door.

"Maybe text me when you get back from the airport," I say. "Let me know how things go."

"Sure," she says, clutching the box of Kleenex.

It's a long five hours, but I finally get a text from Willa.

He didn't say a word. He was acting weird but that's normal for him lately. Sorry for all the drama about nothing. Got my doomed & Burke bag. Yay!

Then: *Dooney.

I stare at the screen for what seems like an hour. I'm feeling relieved and sick to my stomach at the same time. If he didn't tell her, I really should. Why didn't he tell her? I finally text back, Awesome. What else can I say?

CHAPTER 23

I'M UPSTAIRS DOING HOMEWORK WHEN I HEAR THE doorbell ring. Mom's at work. I'm not sure where Trish is. I get up and lean over the top of the stairs. There's banging in the kitchen. "Trish?" I holler.

"Yeah?"

"The door! Get the door!"

"Got it."

I sit back down at my desk. A few seconds later there's a mind-numbing screech that makes me drop my pencil. I push back my chair and run downstairs. When I get to the front hall, I stop short. Trish is sitting on the floor by the door. My eyes do a sweep, trying to process the scene, then my heart does a little lurch. *Is that a breakup basket?* But instantly I know it isn't. It's one of those *other* baskets.

"Look," she whispers.

Holding my breath, I go over and kneel beside her.

"Look," she repeats, holding each basket item up one at a time.

There's a package of diapers, a plastic baby bottle, a pacifier, a jar of baby food, baby wipes, a pregnancy test with "positive" written on the box in red marker. She stops pulling things out when she gets to the pamphlet on Planned Parenthood.

I can't believe what I'm seeing. "Oh my god, Trish."

"Why? Why would they do this to me?" she says. *"Again."*

"Who's they?"

"Those stupid Goodbye Girls!" she spits.

But it wasn't! "Maybe they didn't, though." I put my hand on her shoulder. "Are you sure it couldn't be someone else?"

"Look!" She points.

There's a Goodbye Girl's tag hanging off the handle. It looks exactly like one of ours. *What the hell is going on?*

"And why would you even say that?" she rants. "It's *obviously* them!"

"I don't know," I shrug. "On their website it says that they have nothing to do with these baskets. At least that's what I heard," I quickly add.

"Yeah, *right.*" She sits back on her heels. "Why are you defending them?"

"I'm not. At all. Really." I backpedal. "But why would they lie?"

"Um." She gives me that look like I'm a moron. "Because they're trying to cover their asses. They want to rake in the dough without getting a bad rep." She tosses the pamphlet she's been holding back into the basket. "These Goodbye Girls, they better hope no one finds out who they really are. They'll be *crucified.*"

I don't bother suggesting again that The Goodbye Girls is not at fault. Instead I say, "Trish, you must have *some* idea of who'd be out to get you."

She covers her face with her hands. Her whole body starts to tremble. "No. Nothing this *mean*." After a moment she looks up at me and wipes her nose on the cuff of her hoodie. "I feel sick."

"Here." I slip my arm under hers. "Let me get you to the bathroom."

She snatches her arm back. "Not *that* kind of sick! I feel sick because it has to be someone I know! I mean it has to be, right?"

I don't say anything. We both sit on the floor for a few more minutes.

Finally she gets to her feet. Drawing a shaky breath, she scoops up the basket and heads for the stairs. I follow, licking my suddenly dry lips. In her room, she chucks the basket on the floor then kicks it into her closet.

"Trish," I say, wringing my hands. There's a huge guilty knot in the pit of my stomach. "Can I do anything?"

She spins around. "Promise you won't tell anyone," she says urgently. "I'd just die of embarrassment."

"I swear," I say, shaking my head. "I won't tell a soul."

"Because everyone found out about Olivia and Allan right away...." She wipes her nose again.

That's because they stupidly posted it on Facebook.

"Like I said, I swear I won't tell a soul."

"Thanks." She collapses onto her bed. "I think I wanna be alone right now."

"Are you sure?"

"Yeah. I'm just going to lie down and contemplate the slow painful death of whoever did this."

"Okay." Before I leave, I have to ask. "Trish. You're not pregnant, right?"

Her eyes narrow and something flashes across her face. "No. I'm smart enough to not get myself pregnant."

"Sorry." I clear my throat. "Didn't mean to imply—"

"No, I know," she says. "It's fine."

By the start bell the next morning, everybody at school knows about Trish's pregnancy basket. I see her leave through a side door as I make my way to first class.

Bradley! Get the frig back to school!

CHAPTER 24

WILLA ERASES WHAT SEEMS LIKE AN ENTIRE PAGE of math problems, then blows the eraser dust all over my dining room table. "We're still getting orders," she says. "Even though it says right in bold print that we're not taking any. It's like they can't read."

My phantom ulcer flares up again, as it does any time I hear or think about the business. I've been popping Tums like Tic Tacs.

"It's funny, we're also getting orders for 'revenge' baskets," she adds. "At least that's what they're calling them now."

"*Not* funny," I say.

"No, I know. It's just that you have to marvel. Like, why can't they get it through their heads that it's not us? I'm actually offended that they'd think a nice little business like ours would sink so low."

"I really want to find out who's behind it all."

"I know." She nods. "We're stuck until Bradley comes back to school. How's Trish, by the way?"

"She was pretty upset. She went in this morning, but came right home."

"Wow. She's had a rougher go than most. *Two* baskets."

Sighing, I sweep Willa's eraser mess over the edge of the table. I still feel guilty for everything that Trish is going through. The breakup basket and now this.

"Oh, shoot." Willa slaps her hand on the table. "I meant to bring my new purse to show you. It's absolutely gorgeous."

"I'm sure it is," I say and get out my own sheet of math problems.

"I think that was the reason he wanted us to come to the airport—purely for gift giving," Willa says, sounding all happy. "He got Sean a fabulous Fossil messenger bag. And—" she points her pencil at me—"I can't believe I forgot to tell you this. When we were at his apartment and he was unpacking to get mine and Sean's presents, I saw a Kate Spade box."

"Oh?" I have no idea what that's supposed to mean.

"Mom loves Kate Spade. It's really hard to get here. So whenever Dad travelled to the States, he'd always bring her back a piece of jewellery or something."

A little hiccup catches in my throat. "O-Oh?" I repeat. Mom was sporting a new pair of earrings this morning, but I couldn't ask her about them on account of us not speaking. *Way to be original, Greg.*

"Yeah," Willa continues. "Maybe this other chick was totally just a mid-life crisis thing, or, like, a random hookup, and he's ready to, you know, mend fences or something? Maybe it's like an olive branch for Mom."

I make my face mirror the excitement in hers. "Yeah. Maybe." I want to crawl in a hole and die.

"I can't believe I got so worked up about it. I know everything's gonna be fine." She reaches over and grabs my arm. "What if he comes back home by Christmas?"

"I...uh...uh...I'm really cold. Do you want some hot chocolate?"

"Sure, sure. That'd be great," she says, lost in her dreamy, happy-family thoughts.

"Shit, shit, shit," I mutter under my breath as I turn on the kettle and measure chocolate powder into mugs.

Someone is crashing around in the front hall. I stick my head out the doorway. It's just Trish. The whistle blows on the kettle and I return to my hot chocolate.

"Hey, Willa," I hear Trish say.

"Hey," Willa says back.

"Guess I better get used to seeing you around here a lot more, huh?"

I tilt my head while I stir in the boiling water. *What's that supposed to mean?*

"What's that supposed to mean?" Willa says.

"Well, now that *your* dad's dating *our* mom. I mean, wouldn't it be something if they got married?"

My spoon clatters to the floor and I run into the dining room. "Trish!" I yell.

Willa's eyebrows are knit together. "What are you talking about?" she says to Trish.

"We could be one of those blended families," Trish says, ignoring me. "All livin' together under the same roof. Maybe we'll get our own reality show."

Willa looks over at me, her face white as a ghost. "Lizzie. What is she talking about?"

I open my mouth but no words come out. It's like the air's been sucked out of my lungs.

"Wait." Trish takes a couple steps backward. "Do you not know?" she says to Willa, then she turns to me. "You didn't *tell* her?"

Willa shoves back her chair and stands. "Is she saying that your mom and my dad are…" She holds up both hands. "No. Don't answer. I don't want to know."

"Willa." I finally find my voice. "I wanted so badly to tell you, but—"

"And you *knew*?" she says, giving me a horrified look. "How could you not say anything to me?"

"In Lizzie's defence," Trish says, "she's only known for about a week."

"A *week*?!" Willa shouts.

"Shut up, Trish!" I scream. It's only been five days, but the damage is done.

Trish tiptoes backward out of the room. "I'll just let you two sort it out."

"Willa. I really did want to tell you," I say. "But Mom didn't want me to. She—"

"So?! So what if your mom didn't want you to?!"

"She thought your dad should be the one," I frantically try to explain. "But I told her if he didn't tell you soon, like after his trip, I was going to tell you no matter what."

"Well, he obviously *didn't* tell me," she says sarcastically. "So what's your excuse?"

"I, I tried. I really did. I tried *before* he came home, when I came over before you went to the airport. But you were so upset about the 'homewrecking gold digger,' and your mom, and all the hypotheticals, I—I chickened out."

She pinches her lips together and starts violently packing up her papers and textbooks. "I can't believe you did this. You knew! You knew how I wanted them to get back together."

"Willa," I plead, "that's why I couldn't tell you."

She slings her knapsack over her shoulder and glares at me. "You knew it wasn't going to happen, and you just let me believe it would. Your mom's delusional, you know. Why would he stay with her instead of my mom? My mom is a successful businesswoman. Once she pulls herself together again he'll remember what he's missing." She pauses. "And honestly, if he doesn't come home, I doubt he's going to stay with someone the same age as him. He'll be looking to upgrade."

"Willa," I try again.

"Don't even." She brushes past me. A second later I hear the front door slam.

I slowly lower myself onto the closest dining chair and rest my head face down on my folded arms.

There's the sound of footsteps. "I'm really sorry," Trish says. I feel her hand on my back.

"How could you just come out and say something like that?" I say into the tabletop.

"How was I supposed to know she didn't know? I mean, *seriously*."

"Yeah, well, she didn't."

She snorts. "I don't know what's so bad about it. When I found out, I thought it was kind of cool. Can you imagine Sean as our stepbrother?"

I lift my head, exasperated. "What's bad about it is that Willa thinks I kept it from her."

"Um…you did, didn't you?"

"Gee, thanks, Trish. Could you just go? You've done enough damage for one day." I drop my head back onto my arms.

She sits down beside me. "Look. I meant it when I said I was sorry. I had no idea."

I don't say anything.

"And she'll get over it. I mean, she had to find out some-time, didn't she?"

I keep my head down but manage a shrug.

"Give her a chance to cool down."

"I just wish she hadn't found out like this," I say again into the tabletop.

"I know," Trish says soothingly.

I look up. "Why are you being nice?"

"I kind of feel like it's my fault."

"It *is* your fault. It's *100 percent* your fault."

She raises her eyebrows. "May I remind you, *you're* the one who kept it from her."

My head slams back against the table. "You're right," I whisper.

"How's this," Trish says brightly. "Since I'm *partly* to blame, let me help you get ready for Garret's banquet. It's tomorrow night, right? I just watched this YouTube video on applying makeup. You can be my guinea pig. I promise I'll make you look drop-dead."

"I don't even wanna go anymore," I mumble. I feel like my world has bottomed out.

"Of course you do." She shoves my shoulder. "Isn't this what you always wanted? To be Garret's girlfriend?"

Something in her voice, an edge, makes me sneak a side-ways peek. Maybe I'm imagining things. I realize how hard it must be for her to make this offer.

"Thanks, Trish," I say. "I'd really like that."

CHAPTER 25

"HOW ABOUT ONE OF THESE?" TRISH HAS A BUNCH of her dresses spread out over my bed.

I can't exactly tell her what I'm thinking—*Waaay too slutty*—so I say, "They're nice, but they don't really seem to be me, you know?"

In a perfect world it would be Willa here, standing in my room, bossing me around, telling me what to wear, trying to create a smokey eye, but she hasn't spoken to me since she stormed out of the dining room the other day.

So Trish is here instead, offering to help me get ready, all because she feels guilty about letting the cat out of the bag. I'm the one who should feel guilty. Just a few weeks ago, Trish probably thought it would be *her* getting ready for the football banquet.

"Trish? Are you sure you want to do this?" I ask. "I can probably handle it."

"Nah. I got nothin' better to do." She clears her throat, smiles tightly, and turns to face the dress display. "So none of these?"

"I don't think so." My voice sounds really small.

"I guess you can wear that turquoise dress," she says unenthusiastically. "The one you wore for the grade nine graduation."

"I love that dress. The colour makes me look like I have a tan when I don't. And it was expensive."

"Yeah, yeah, I remember." She presses her lips together, gathers up her dresses, and tosses them on my desk chair. "Mom went with all her coupons and scratch cards, practically beat up the sales clerk, and got it for like, five bucks."

"It was a bit more than *five*."

"Not much," she says. "Haul it out so I can match it to your makeup and nail polish."

I go to the closet and lift out the hanger.

Trish spends the next hour layering on primer, foundation, eyeliner, shadow, mascara, brow gel, powder, blush, bronzer, lip liner, and lip gloss. You name it, I have it on my face. The whole time, she gossips about her friends. The stories are nonsensical and have no point, but it's the longest conversation we've ever had.

Next she does my nails in a colour that's pretty much the same as my dress. While it dries, she starts on my hair. She flattens, crimps, waves, curls—I swear she has six appliances going at the same time.

She gets frustrated when one piece of hair won't go the way she wants it to. I hear her cursing under her breath.

"Are you okay?" I say. "I can just pin that piece back."

"I'm fine!" She slams the curling iron down on the dresser. Then she takes a deep breath and picks it up again. "I'm fine," she repeats calmly. She wraps the hair tightly around the shaft, yanking on my scalp hard enough to make my eyes water. After a minute she slides the shaft out. "Much better."

When she's all done, she stands back to assess her work. "Not bad," she says, tilting her head.

"Can I look?"

"Not yet. Don't move." She leaves and comes back a second later. "Here we go." She holds up a skinny bejewelled hairband. "The finishing touch." She slips it onto my head, tucks it behind my ears, then turns me toward the mirror. "Voila."

It takes a second for me to recognize the reflection. I think there was a part of me that expected her to sabotage my makeup and I'd end up looking like a clown. And maybe I would kind of deserve it. But I don't look like a clown. I look good. Not just good—great.

"Thanks, Trish. You did an amazing job."

"No worries." She begins collecting her stuff off the dresser and packing them back in her makeup suitcase. "Let me know if you need help with your dress."

"I should be good, thanks."

"Do you want me to take a picture for Mom? She's not going to be home before you leave."

Oh god. It reminds me of when I made the same offer to her, right before she left for the fall semi-formal. With Garret.

"Uh...no thanks." Also, I didn't tell Mom I was going to the football team's banquet. I told her I volunteered to *work* the football team's banquet. I'm still not sure what she'd think about me going out with Garret. Mom hasn't mentioned him, so obviously Trish hasn't said anything to her about it. She doesn't really confide in Mom.

She shrugs. "All right, then. Have fun. Don't do anything I wouldn't do."

"Yeah. Thanks again, Trish."

I make sure I'm waiting on the front porch when Garret comes to get me. I don't want him to come to the door. *Talk about awkward.*

I get a little breathless when I see him. He's wearing a suit and looks like he's about twenty-five. And gorgeous.

He takes a step back. His eyes sweep over me, up and down. "You look...off the hook."

I feel my cheeks get warm. "That's good, right?" I joke.

The banquet is at the Future Inn just down the street from the school. The room and food are done up pretty fancy considering it's all high school kids with a few coaches thrown in.

The evening consists mostly of speeches, awards, and a lot of bro-hugging and back-slapping, even though they didn't have that great a season. That seems to be all forgotten tonight.

During the speeches, Garret casually drapes his arm over the back of my chair. He's taken off his suit jacket and rolled up his shirt sleeves. I can feel his skin against the back of my neck.

Garret receives the Most Sportsmanlike award. Which I guess is the football version of Miss Congeniality. Before he goes up to get it, he looks right at me, smiles, and squeezes my hand. In his acceptance speech, I'm half expecting him to thank me for making it all possible. Of course he doesn't, but in my imagination he does.

The other girls, or dates, are outwardly nice, but I can tell they are all wondering about me, wondering what the hell I'm doing here with Garret. I don't know how many know I'm Trish's sister, but I know some do, and I suspect they're sharing a few comments behind my back. I don't care though. I know I look smokin', and I'm with the most popular guy there.

After three glasses of punch I need a bathroom break. I'm in one of the stalls when I hear some girls come in. There's the sound of water running, the clicking and snapping of compacts and assorted makeup cases opening and closing, then—

"Can you believe that slut-bag came here? With her sister's ex-boyfriend?"

"I know, right? Doesn't she know that Trish's baby is probably Garret's?"

"I mean, *duh.*"

"God. That'll make for some interesting family Christmas dinner convo."

I don't move a muscle, not even to breathe. Thankfully my cheeks and neck bursting into flames don't make a sound. I close my eyes and pray for them to leave. They finally do. I remain in the stall for a few moments to settle myself down. I pull open the door and check my makeup in the mirror. There's a tear hanging precariously on the rim of each eye. Tears of anger? I blink and let them fall, then quickly dab them away. I adjust my hairband, put on a brave face, and return to the table in the banquet room. Their coach is giving another speech.

"Everything okay?" Garret whispers in my ear.

"Yeah," I whisper back. "Fine."

When it's all over, Garret says, "Everyone's going back to Josh's to hang out. Do you wanna come?"

Not for all the money in the world. And also, it doesn't fit in with my plan to be home and de-glamourized before

Mom gets back, so I won't have to explain why I'm all dressed up.

"Um, not to sound like a downer," I say, "but I should get home. I have an essay due Monday." Lie. "But *you* go, of course."

He frowns. "Are you sure? I'd really like you to come."

"Totally sure. Go celebrate. Plus you'll have more fun if I'm not there."

"Why would you say that?"

"Because I don't really know anybody, and if I'm there you'll just be worrying whether I'm having a good time."

"Oh." He thinks about this, then shrugs. "I don't have to go. It's not that big a deal."

He's so nice.

We go back and forth for another minute until he finally gives in and agrees to go without me.

He drives me home and walks me to the front step. As we stand under the porch light I silently pray Trish is up in her room, which is on the side of the house.

"I had a really good time," Garret says, facing me.

I make myself shove the bathroom incident to the back of my brain. "Yeah, me too." My voice is all shaky because I'm nervous. He's going to kiss me, I know it. I lick my lips to get ready.

He leans in. It's like everything's in slow motion. The kiss is brief but not too brief. It's moist but not slobbery. His lips taste like the molten lava cake we had for dessert. It's what I've been imagining since grade three. All in all, it's perfect. Just like him. I'm having visions of kissing him all over New York, us walking hand in hand through Times Square, making out at the top of the Empire State Building.

I feel all light and spacey when I walk in the front door. Trish is just coming down the stairs. She didn't see anything!

"Hey," she says. "How was it?"

"Good. Nice." I nod. "Nice and good." I try to sound toned down, like it was just *okay.*

"Your makeup stayed set." She tilts her head like she's studying me. "Your lip gloss is a little smudged, though."

I gasp and raise a hand to my lips.

"Just teasing," she smiles, but it doesn't quite reach her eyes.

"Well, uh, thanks again for helping me get ready, Trish." I'm uncomfortable talking any more about my night, and I can't imagine she really wants to hear about it. I start up the stairs.

"Hey, Lizzie," she calls after me.

I turn. "Yeah?"

"You do look really pretty." She says it as if she's just noticed for the first time.

"Uh…thanks, Trish."

Up in my room I undress and sit down at my desk. It takes about four makeup wipes to get all my makeup off. The makeup Trish laboured to put on me.

I pull my phone out of my purse and check for messages. I'm only looking for one from Willa. There isn't one. I should be texting her all about the night, the banquet, the bathroom. She would want to know every single detail; she'd have a fit if she even *suspected* I was leaving anything out. Then I could tell her how I'm feeling, about how maybe it's not such a great idea, me seeing Garret. Then she would tell me I'm crazy, that everything happens for a reason, and she'd offer to beat up the bathroom girls, and so on and so on. We would talk more about our plans for New York, figure out how to make sure we got to room together. And I haven't even told her about my idea to sneak off to Greenwich Village, where Taylor Swift lives. I've even researched Taylor's favourite place to eat—The Spotted Pig. Then I would describe the kiss and the banquet in detail all over again.

I toss the phone on the bed. She probably didn't even remember it was tonight.

CHAPTER 26

I'M WALKING DOWN THE HALL TO ART WHEN MRS. Spencer, the vice-principal, taps me on the shoulder. "Ms. Turner. Mr. Scott would like to see you in his office."

My breath catches. "W-what?"

"Hurry along," she says. "I'll let Mrs. Devane know you'll be late."

Telling myself not to panic, I go to the front office. "Mrs. Spencer said Mr. Scott wants to see me," I say to the secretary.

She gestures for me to go on back. Mr. Scott's door is open. I step inside and close it behind me.

He's sitting at his desk, papers and folders spread out in front of him.

"Have a seat, Ms. Turner," he says. "Can I call you Lizzie? That's what you go by, right?"

I nod and sit. *Oh god, oh god, oh god.*

He comes out from behind his desk and sort of half-sits on the corner, letting his leg swing free. "Do you know why I called you in here?"

I clutch the armrests. "No, sir."

"Let's get to the heart of the matter, shall we?" He doesn't wait for me to answer. "I suppose you are familiar with this Goodbye Girls business. It's been the talk of the school lately."

I feel my heart rate speed up. "Yes. I've heard of it."

"Well, apparently these people are branching out." He looks at me with raised eyebrows. "As I'm sure you're well aware."

As I'm well aware? Why would I be well aware? But I go ahead and nod again.

"They've delivered baskets containing some rather disturbing items to a number of students, including your sister."

Of course. Trish, my sister...phew. "Right," I say. "It was awful." *Did he call me in to offer up a list of Trish's possible enemies?*

"The thing is, this morning I found a letter slipped under my door saying you and Willa Carlson are the ones responsible for it all."

It's like the air is sucked out of the room. "What?"

"Now I know the petty differences that go on between students, but this—"

"It wasn't us!"

He holds up a hand. "I understand your distress, but I had no choice but to call you in to explore all the possibilities. I mean, either you and Willa *are* responsible, or someone mistakenly *believes* you are, or someone has an axe to grind."

"It wasn't us," I repeat. It's all I can think to say.

Sighing, he strokes his chin. "Unfortunately, Ms. Carlson is absent today, but I didn't think we should put off having this talk."

"She must be sick." I automatically cover for her.

"Yes, I'm sure she is." He reaches around behind him and picks up some folders.

My heart rate speeds up again, thumping in double time, so loud I can hear it in my ears. "Honestly, Mr. Scott. We didn't do this. Willa would say the same thing if she was here."

He nods. "I've spent much of the morning speaking with your and Ms. Carlson's teachers, and after looking at your records—they're both exemplary, by the way—I confess I'm inclined to believe you."

My breathing evens out a bit.

"Not that I haven't been wrong before," he continues. "But I find, as do your teachers, that this type of behaviour would be highly out of character for you two."

I'm afraid to agree in case he thinks I'm agreeing that's he's been wrong before, so I say nothing.

"And I find it hard to imagine you would deliver such a basket to your own sister," he says dryly.

"No, no. I wouldn't." I shake my head.

"But Lizzie, I must ask, do you have any idea who would? Or any idea what this is all about?"

"No," I whisper.

He sits quietly for a moment, thinking. "What I'd really like to see happen is you, Willa, Trisha…" He leans over to glance at another folder on his desk. "Allan, and Olivia, come in here to see if we can get to the bottom of this. See if we can discover some common thread that connects the five of you to this Goodbye Girls business."

"Oh…um, can we really be sure it's The Goodbye Girls, though? Like, maybe it's some copycat, some random person."

He frowns. "Why would you think that?"

"I heard, uh…that's what it says on their website."

"Yes, well, you can't believe everything's that's on the internet, and also they could be protecting themselves."

"I guess," I say, because I can't come across too pro–The Goodbye Girls. "Regrettably, neither Allan or Olivia have come in to see me. Only your sister has. She's actually the one who told me about the other two." He shakes his head, an expression of frustration on his face. "The police should be involved in this. These incidents are beyond bullying; they're out-and-out harassment, and this school has zero tolerance for that sort of thing."

The mention of police makes me dizzy even though I'm sitting down.

"I'm hoping the other victims come in of their own accord, but we're running out of time. Perhaps you, your sister, or Willa can nudge them a little?"

"Oh, I, uh, don't really know them."

"Well, we're all going to have to get together at some point, definitely before Christmas break. That only gives us a few days." He stands and returns to his desk chair. "You're free to go, Lizzie. If you think of anything, or learn of anything, please come see me immediately."

He doesn't have to dismiss me twice. I'm out of there like a shot. Rushing down the hall, I duck under the stairs by the guidance office and press my back against the concrete wall. I need a minute to think in private and have a nervous breakdown. It'll be quiet here until next class change.

Should I tell Willa I was hauled into the principal's office? Will she even care? She'll care when I tell her she's probably next. And she'll care if Mr. Scott drags the police into this. *All* the rogue baskets say they're from The Goodbye Girls. How do we prove that they're not? Or do the police have to prove that they are? *I don't know, I don't know.* One thing I *do* know is, a disclaimer on our website isn't enough. That doesn't really prove anything.

God. If the police get involved, they have special equipment that can examine or track computer stuff and whatever, even if it's deleted. They'll know we're the original Goodbye Girls in no time. They'll probably ask for Willa's computer. That'll erase any doubt. Then what happens?

I drag my hands down my face, stretching the skin tight over my bones. *Okay, Lizzie. Time to get it together!* I'm going to find out who's doing this. By myself. And I'm starting today. Because I don't have any other choice. Like Mr. Scott said, we're running out of time.

That afternoon I move through the halls, going from class to class, suspiciously eyeing everyone I pass. The result is the same as the last time I did it. There's no one. I mean, there are tons of people who might be out to get Trish or even Olivia, who's kind of annoying. I don't really know much about Bradley or Claire, but I know Allan's just a big teddy bear. There is no connection between them all, and nothing that explains why me and Willa are being hung out to dry.

My head hurts from thinking so hard. I'm in a kind of brain-dead trance as I get my stuff out of my locker. That's when a thought occurs to me. Willa and I talked about whether maybe the recipients of the rogue baskets were collateral damage, all just part of making us look bad. But what if our business *is* the collateral damage? Maybe someone's seeking revenge on their enemies and just using The Goodbye Girls to cover their tracks.

I spend the evening trying to remember everyone we delivered baskets to. I write each name down—I hardly know any of them. I know I'm missing tonnes, especially the ones from the other high schools. I also write down the people who received the rogue baskets. There's no connection that I can see. Not between each other, or to us, or between our basket people and the rogue basket people. The only red flag, if I can even call it that, is Amy. I mean, she saw me, but did she recognize me? And even if she did, I can't imagine she'd do anything like this. It makes no sense. Nothing does.

CHAPTER 27

I'M EXHAUSTED.

As I walk down the hall at school, I swear the lockers are moving in a wave pattern. I zone out through English, my eyes glued to Willa's empty chair. Maybe she really is sick.

Using my entire body, I push myself out through the swinging bathroom door. Then, like a bright light at the end of a dark tunnel, I see him. Bradley. He's wrestling Jordan Short right by the cafeteria doors. As I get closer it becomes apparent he's not actually wrestling, he's trying to give him a wet willy. *Looks like he's recovered from his mono.*

I keep on going. I can't rush at him and start bombarding him with questions. I need a plan. Because I still have the same problem. How do I ask him questions about his email to The Goodbye Girls without revealing that *I'm* The Goodbye Girls? Or one of them anyway.

I devote my entire French class to devising a plan.

I figure it would be best if there was some way we could look at his email account together, so that's what I'm shooting for. Depending on how quickly, or hopefully *slowly*, Willa sent a confirmation, there's a chance it's still there, attached to the original order request. Though if it was, Bradley probably would have seen it by now, wouldn't he? Maybe not… most students don't ever use their school accounts. I can't remember the last time I was on mine.

I come up with this pathetic idea to tell him I got an email from him telling me he likes me. And he'll be all like, "What?!" and I'll be all like, "Well, it's from your email address. If not you, then who?" and he'll probably say, "No clue," and I'll say, "We should look at your account because I replied, so the thread will still be there and maybe you'd be able to tell who sent it."

Then, if Willa's confirmation email *is* there. I could be all like, "You hired The Goodbye Girls?" and he'll be all pissed and out of his mind to find out who's messing with him. Hopefully he'll be able to remember someone he gave his address and password to, or someone who was using his computer when his account would have been open.

It's a long shot and totally convoluted. And there's also one major flaw. If he's on the ball at all, he will just say, "Show me the email on your phone." I'll say, "I don't get my emails sent to my phone," which is a lie, and we'll have to go to a computer terminal anyway. I'll make something up from there. Maybe I can't remember my password…However it goes down, I'm coming away with a list of suspects.

"Hey Bradley! Wait up!" I run up behind him in the hall.

He turns. "Huh?"

"Hi. You probably don't even know me." I pretend to be flustered and out of breath. "But I was just wondering if I can talk to you for a sec."

He says, "Sure." He doesn't look very sure.

"Well, this is a bit embarrassing..." I fiddle with my watch strap and stare at the floor.

"Hey, wait. Aren't you Trish's sister?"

"Yup." I smile brightly. "That's my claim to fame."

"Yeah, thought so." He points a finger at me. "You kind of look like her."

I can't bring myself to say thanks, so I just hold my smile.

"She's in my Business Tech. She's majorly hot."

I screw up my face. *Ew.*

"But she's really smart too," he adds quickly, as if he realizes what he said may have been inappropriate. "She was my partner for the midterm project and she totally rocked it."

"Yes, yes," I say. "She's an absolute genius." *Stay on track.* But then something clicks in my head. "Wait. Did you say Trish was your partner for a project?"

"Yeah."

"In Business Tech?"

"Yeah."

I have a vague recollection of Trish saying something about that. "Your class is in the computer lab, right? Like you do it all on computers?"

"Yeah." He starts looking bored.

Just then two guys come running around the corner. They jump on Bradley, piggyback style, and they all end up on the floor. I have to step back so I don't get knocked over.

"Gym! Five minutes, shithead!" one of them shouts. The other puts Bradley in a headlock and violently gives him a noogie. After that, they both run off.

"Look, I gotta get to practice," Bradley says. "Is that what you wanted to talk about? Business Tech?"

"No, I, uh." I try to focus my thoughts, but my mind keeps racing ahead. Could it be? Could it be Trish? No. Just because she worked on a project with him doesn't mean she could get into his email. How could that even happen?

He gives me a strange look. "Are you okay?"

"Yeah. I'm good." But the racing in my mind doesn't stop. It keeps going back to the same thing. Bradley said it himself. Trish is smart. How smart? I have to find out.

My original plan has completely gone sideways. I have to wing it. I straighten up, push my hair back from my face, and like a miracle, from nowhere it comes to me. "No. I didn't want to talk about Business Tech," I say, whipping a notepad out of my knapsack. "I'm collecting information for the office. There's been a security breach involving a number of student email addresses." I'm shocked at how much I sound like I know what I'm talking about.

He scrunches up his nose. "I hardly use it. Just for school shit—homework and stuff."

"But do you allow other people access to your account? Your girlfriend? One of those guys who just threw you on the floor? A class partner, perhaps?" I hint.

"No, never." He shakes his head.

"Good." *Phew.*

"Oh, just a second." He starts nodding. "Trish used my account when we were working on our project."

"W-What?" *No. I so wanted to be wrong.*

"Yeah." He frowns. "She'd already closed down her computer and needed to email part of the project to herself."

I momentarily rest my shoulder against the wall. I need it to hold me up.

He shrugs. "But no big deal, right? That wouldn't have anything to do with anything, would it?"

"Uh…" My mouth feels dry. I lick my lips over and over again until I'm able to make words come out. "We don't recommend you allow *anyone* access to your account," I say quietly while trying to sound official, like the words are straight from office administration. Then I do some fake writing. Bradley cranes his neck, trying to see what I'm putting down, but I hold my notebook closer to my chest.

Sighing loudly, he starts rocking back and forth on his heels, looking over his shoulder toward the gym.

I know I have to keep it together and finish this up before I lose him. "One last thing. For security purposes, and so we can eliminate yours from the list of corrupted accounts, could you please verify your email account address and password?" I hold my breath, praying he won't think twice about me asking for his password. That he wants so badly to get to the damn gym, he'll give me anything I ask for.

"Yeah, sure. Bfp675663@student.ednet.ns.ca." He starts walking backward. "X1C6Y8."

I blow out a huge gush of air while I scribble it all down. "If you don't get an email from the office, then you're all clear," I say, but when I look up he's long gone.

Heading for the library, I find an empty terminal and sit down. I log into the computer and open the student email page. Then I type in his email and password and wait for the page to load. I'm not even sure what I'm looking for—I guess anything that points to Trish. I'm still hoping I'm wrong, but I can't shake the feeling that I'm not. I know Trish is smart. Smarter than most give her credit for.

The first thing I plan to look for is the confirmation email from The Goodbye Girls. There's a good chance Trish, or *whoever*, didn't even know there was a confirmation email, and therefore wouldn't have waited for it. If it's there, the original order request will be there as well.

His account pops up. There's nothing in his inbox except a few emails from teachers, "Missing Homework" in the subject lines. Definitely no order confirmation. Willa must have responded right away, while whoever was still in Bradley's account, and it got deleted. So I go to Bradley's deleted items folder, hoping it's still there. It's not. Nothing is. It's been emptied.

I drum my fingernails on the table. Then I stop. *I wonder...*

I click on the sent folder. There it is, our email address, and in the subject line, "ORDER." This is the email supposedly sent to us from Bradley, ordering a basket for Claire. I didn't need the confirmation email after all. Everything's here—the filled-out questionnaire and the comment section requesting us to enclose the sealed letter, the one containing the photo. I check the date and time on the email: *November 22, 3:09 P.M.*. I drum my fingers some more. Last block on Mondays...what does Trish have? *How much you wanna bet it's Business Tech?*

I look at the date again. We would have scheduled the delivery for that Thursday or Friday. And Willa would have sent that info with the confirmation. Then I remember, it was Friday, because Simon Clark's party was the next night. That's when Garret texted me to come over. It was also the morning after that party that Trish barged into my room looking for the Advil, and *that's* when she mentioned she was partners with Bradley. The timing works. I pull out my phone and take a picture of the computer screen. And as backup, I forward the email to my own address.

I run home, my anger propelling me forward at a speed I didn't know I was capable of. But then as my legs tire and my pace slows, my anger does too. I mean, am I really that surprised? I know this has to be about Garret. I guess I just can't believe how she was able to pull this all off without me suspecting. I can't believe how much she wanted to see me suffer. And I can't believe that she was willing to humiliate herself just to get one step closer to her goal. Now *that's* dedication.

God, I feel so stupid!

My phone chirps and I jerk to a stop. *Willa?* But no, it's a text from Garret.

Keep missing u at school did you get yur essay done?

Right. I lied the night of the banquet and said I had an essay due.

Yup, I text back. Why stop lying now? Hopefully see you soon :)

I stare at the message for a moment, wondering if I should have written more. I shake my head. I just can't think about him till I get all this other stuff sorted out.

I still manage to make it to my front door in record time, beating Trish. I go straight to the kitchen and whip open the cupboard door. It's where Mom has our class schedules taped up.

My eyes zero in on Trish's schedule. Monday, to be exact. I slide my finger down the page, stopping on A block, last class of the day, 2:20–3:20. Business Technology.

CHAPTER 28

I SIT ON THE EDGE OF TRISH'S BED AND WAIT. MY palms are sweaty. I wipe them on her duvet. Mom's at work, so except for the occasional whoosh of a car passing on the street, everything is quiet and still.

Rarely allowed entrance into Trish's room, I take a look around. Mounds of clothes litter the floor, and more clothes are strewn over every piece of available furniture. Makeup, assorted empty water bottles, and Tim Horton's cardboard cups clutter her dresser top. Then I see the bejewelled hairband she lent me hanging off the corner of an open drawer.

It was all a lie. There was no sisterly bonding. We weren't becoming friends. She was acting. It was all part of her plan.

She takes Drama, too.

I hear the front door open then close, the sound of stuff being dumped on the hall bench. My body stiffens into battle mode. I practiced everything I wanted to say. I can't wait to tell her exactly what I think of her.

"Hey." She doesn't seem surprised to find me in her room. She tosses a calculator and textbook onto the bed next to me. "I don't suppose you know anything about grade twelve Calculus. God. I can't believe they make you take it for nursing. Like I'm ever going to actually *use* it."

I watch her peel off her hoodie. The static makes a bunch of her hairs stand up, spray out like peacock feathers. She smoothes them down. "So what's up? You're never in here."

"I'm never invited."

She raises her eyebrows. I think she can tell by my tone that something's up.

"Look Trish, I—"

"Let me guess. You wanna borrow something." She smiles and wags a finger at me. "Just because I offered to lend you stuff for the banquet doesn't mean you get the run of my closet now."

She's acting so normal, nice even…but I can't let that distract me. I take a deep breath and square my shoulders. "Trish, I know it's you."

"Know it's me, what?" She drapes her hoodie over the back of her desk chair.

"That it's you sending those baskets, trying to get me in shit."

She stays quiet for a second. "Oh. That."

"Yeah!" I snap. "*That!*"

More seconds pass. "How'd you figure it out?"

"Bradley," I say. "He said you'd used his email account."

"Ah, yes, Bradley," she mutters.

"You deleted everything except the sent folder," I add.

"Oh." She sits down at her desk. "Sucks to be me."

Her whole demeanour fills me with disbelief and confusion. She's not shocked, she's not worried. She's *certainly* not sorry. Everything I'd rehearsed is suddenly out the window, a giant mind sweep. The only thing I can manage to get out is, "Why?"

"Why did I do it?"

"Yeah."

Her eyes darken to an inky black. I'm pretty sure she wants to rip my face off.

"You stole my boyfriend," she says through clenched teeth.

I knew it! "No I didn't!"

"You sat back and watched me be all in love with him." She glares at me and shakes her head. "Bet you loved every minute of it."

"*What?*"

"Not only that," she says. "You knew I spent two hundred bucks on a watch for him for Christmas. You even let me wear your sweater on my last ever date with him. You were having a *grand* ol' time, weren't you?"

"I didn't *let* you wear it. You *took* it!"

"And all along you knew he was going to break up with me! You knew how I felt about him, and you let me go on living in some...some *dream* world!"

Déjà vu. It's basically what Willa said to me when she found out I knew about my mom and her dad. She was right. They both are, as much as it stings. But both situations had extenuating circumstances. I struggle to get some words out. "Well, I was trapped. I couldn't say anything, I...."

Her cheeks flush and her chest heaves up and down.

"I didn't *steal* him!" I shout.

"Oh, puh-lease. People couldn't *wait* to tell me how you two were all over each other at the wake-a-thon."

"We *weren't*." But my voice doesn't come out very forceful.

"And always all cozy, tucked in a corner at Tim's!"

"That was *once*!" I'm back to shouting.

"So you admit it!"

"No! We were just getting something to drink after we went fundraising."

A loud bang sounds over our fighting. We both stop and look at each other. "Mom's home," I whisper.

Trish goes and peeks out the window. "It's just the wind. It knocked over the Mitchells' green bin."

I let out a breath. "Like I was saying." I try to keep my voice calm and even. "It was a drink after fundraising. To warm up. He had a coffee and I had a hot chocolate. That's all."

"Isn't that precious. You remember every detail," Trish says bitterly, sitting back down at her desk. "Is that what you had when you went to that movie at Park Lane, too?"

My eyes widen.

"Yeah," she smirks. "Olivia's brother works concessions. He knows Garret. Did it make it more thrilling? All the sneaking around behind my back?"

Now *my* cheeks flush red. "We went to *one* movie. Nothing happened." What else could I say?

She leans back in her chair, looking pleased with herself.

"But then I came and told you," I say defensively. "I told you he asked me out."

"Only because you *had* to. Because you were going to the banquet with all *my* friends."

Neither of us say anything for a minute. *Okay, maybe I didn't go about things in the best possible way….* Then my anger kicks in again, but this time it's directed at myself. Why am

I feeling guilty? It should be *her*. She should be begging me for forgiveness.

"So because you *think* I stole your boyfriend, which I *didn't,* by the way, you masterminded this"—I sweep my arms though the air—"whole plan to ruin my life?"

"Not your *whole* life." She shrugs. "I just wanted to take that trip away from you. I'm so sick of you getting everything you want."

"Wow, Trish." My eyes fill with water, which makes me even madder at myself.

"What? You make it sound like I'm crazy and you don't deserve it or something."

"I *don't*! I asked you if you were okay with me and Garret. *More* than once. All you had to do was say no!"

"I couldn't do that," she says tightly.

"Well then, that makes you an idiot."

She gives me that look again, like she wants to rip my face off.

"Shit, Trish. How much time, money, and aggravation did it cost you to pull all this off?"

"I admit it," she says. "It wasn't easy. But nothing I did worked. All I needed was *one* person to lodge a formal complaint and force Mr. Scott into taking some action. Was that too much to ask?"

I don't bother answering.

"I wanted him to make an announcement or something. Bring people in for questioning. Something that would scare the shit out of you and make you shut everything down. Something that would cut off your money supply."

"You are one jealous, vindictive bitch."

My name-calling has no effect. She slides an elastic off her wrist and puts her hair into a ponytail "But then you *didn't* deliver the basket to Claire. Allan couldn't be *bothered* to go to the principal—he was too busy being famous. And Olivia…Jesus! She *said* she was going to the principal, but she only talked to the guidance counsellor. She ended up joining Weight Watchers with her mom—said it was a wake-up call, and a good time to get healthy and lose some weight before prom."

"Trish. These people are your *friends*."

"These people are *not* my friends. Claire is a self-righteous little bitch. She wanted Bradley to switch when he got paired up with me. Told him I would probably try to steal him from her. As *if*. And Olivia's a two-faced backstabber. She was texting Garret behind my back the whole time we were going out."

"What about Allan? He wouldn't hurt a flea."

"Right. Allan," she scoffs. "Remember when Mom used to babysit him after school?"

"Yeah."

"One afternoon when I was at Brownies, he drew nipples and pubic hair on all my Barbies in permanent marker. Ruined! They were all *ruined*." She closes her eyes. "It was too embarrassing to show Mom, so he got away with it."

"Trish! That was like ten years ago!"

"Yeah. So?"

I shake my head sadly. "I can't believe it. You're right. You *literally* have no friends."

"I play the role, though. That's all you need in high school. Everyone's so superficial. No one's really friends with anyone. The sooner you learn that, the better.

I gawk at her. "What's *wrong* with you?"

"There's nothing wrong with me." She pulls a makeup wipe from her drawer and drags it down her face. "In six months I'm outta here, and 99 percent of these people I'll never have to see again."

"It's like you're soulless," I whisper.

She ignores my comment. "Like I said, nothing was working. You didn't shut down your business, you just took a *break* for a while. And Mr. Scott was still oblivious. I had to do something drastic. Take matters into my own hands."

"So you sent that basket to yourself." I give her a slow clap. "Bravo on the Oscar-worthy performance."

"Genius, huh?"

"And you're all...*okay* with people thinking you're pregnant?"

She shrugs. "I don't care what people think about me."

"Bullshit. That's *all* you care about."

"No." She frowns as she studies all the black goo on the wipe. "See, you think you know me, but you don't."

"No kidding," I say.

"I'm not stupid. I knew exactly what would happen. Tell a couple of blabbermouths about the basket I got, and the word would be out in a matter of minutes. Everyone would think I was the revenge baskets' new target, that someone was out to get me, and they'd all rally around me, pour on their fake sympathy—poor little me—which is exactly what happened."

I sit there, staring at her. She really wasn't lying when she said I didn't know her.

"I mean," she continues. "Time will prove that obviously I'm *not* pregnant...but I guess they might assume I had an abortion. Whatever." She shrugs.

I keep staring.

"I want you to know, though," she says, tilting her head. "There was a moment when I *did* have a change of heart."

I snort. You can't have a change of heart without a heart.

"It's true. It was the night you went to Garret's banquet. You looked so nice. You were so excited. And when you got home you were so happy. You were like a little Cinderella."

I feel my lip curling into a snarl. *You're such a liar.*

"You thanked me again for helping you get ready," she says. "I started to feel sort of bad. Started to feel that maybe what I was doing to you was kind of shitty. I know how long you've liked Garret. Since elementary. I get it. Maybe you were even mad when I snagged him. Not that you had any right to be. Anyway, by the time I had my epiphany, it was too late. I'd already cried to Mr. Scott and delivered the tip-off letter." Her phone buzzes from inside her knapsack on the bed next to me. I dare her with my eyes to answer it. She doesn't move.

"Yeah. The letter," I say. "Why would you drag Willa into all this? You didn't even know if she had anything to do with it."

Her mouth hangs open. "Oh, come on! There's no way you could have pulled this off on your own. Who else would be helping you? You don't have any other friends."

I set my jaw and breathe heavily through my nose. I feel like a bull getting ready to charge.

"Plus, I know she thinks I'm a waste of space," she adds. "Taking her down with you was just a bonus."

"Okay, just so I understand. Taking the trip away from me wasn't enough. You had to screw over my best friend as well as make it so the entire school thinks that we're money-grubbing scum. Because I'm sure part of your plan is to leak the fact that Mr. Scott got a letter naming me and Willa." I fold my arms and wait for her to answer.

She doesn't.

"You know, Trish. Like your 'pregnancy.' Eventually people are going to know that it wasn't me and Willa. And that it wasn't The Goodbye Girls."

"Why? Because you say so? You can deny it all you want. Doesn't mean they have to believe you. Plus, no one's going to buy that I sent that basket to myself. It was pretty harsh."

"I'll make them," I say.

"Good *luck*." She balls up her makeup wipe and throws it in the wastebasket.

For what feels like the hundredth time, I can only stare at her and wonder, *Where the hell did you come from?* I slide down to the end of the bed so I'm closer to her. "Actually, you better hope that they don't," I say quietly. "*Especially* Mr. Scott. He's hardcore serious. He's getting the police involved." *At least he wants to.*

At last I get a reaction. She blinks a few times as she digests the information. Her cheeks don't have much colour anymore. "The police?"

"Yeah," I nod. "And if I can convince Mr. Scott that you're the one behind this, it'll go on your permanent record. You can kiss any chance of a scholarship goodbye." I make little waving motions with my hand. "You know the school has zero tolerance for bullying." I sound like Mr. Scott. "And they have *less* than zero tolerance for harassment."

"Harassment?"

"That's what Mr. Scott's calling it. What would *you* call it?"

She doesn't say anything, but I can hear her breathing. It's different. Slower.

"I should give you the heads up," I say. "I took a photo of Bradley's sent folder. It has the date and time. It's during your class together, you know, when you were project partners? Easy to check. And I'm sure I can get Bradley to tell Mr. Scott you were using his email account. Once I lay everything out for him, connect all the dots, tell him every-thing *you* just told me…"

Again I wait, but she still says nothing. I get up and go to the door. Touching the handle, I pause and turn. "How did you figure out The Goodbye Girls was me and Willa?"

"Girl Guide cookies," she says flatly. "I took five bucks from your wallet. I saw the receipt for *Love Actually*. The anniversary edition. Thanks for the splurge, by the way." She spits the last few words.

"I feel sorry for you, Trish. Because I'm going to prove to Mr. Scott that it's you. There's going to be no scholarship, and you're going to be stuck here in Halifax, having to make nice with all your *fake* friends, if they'll even speak to you after they find out what you've done, for god knows how long."

Before I leave, I take a last look back. I see Trish staring straight ahead at nothing, her face like stone.

I don't leave my room for the rest of the day. There's no noise from down the hall, so I'm not sure Trish has left her room either. Though her reasons are probably different from mine. Me, I've been spending the hours trying to make sense of what just happened. I can't. I can't figure out how it went so wrong. We were both raised under the same roof, by the same mom, with the same values, rules, and beliefs. How could we have turned out so different?

All these injustices that Trish imagines have been committed against her, they're just that—imagined. And the fact that her biggest beef is with me, that she's actually jealous...of course, she didn't use those exact words, but still. It's insane. I've spent my entire life jealous of *her*. I thought she had it all going on. Apparently not. I could never have guessed in a million years how unhappy she truly was—*is*. It's weird, though; I don't think she even realizes she's unhappy.

It's almost dark. As I reach over to turn on my bedside lamp, there's a knock on my door.

Mom sticks her head in. "Hey," she says.

I make eye contact, but that's all. Nothing much has changed as far as how our conversations go.

She sets down a mug on my dresser. "The house feels extra cold tonight. I made some hot chocolate. I put a glob of Nutella in just the way you like." She gives me a hopeful look.

"Thanks," I say and turn my attention to some random scribbler that happens to be lying on my bed.

I hear her move into the room and sit on my chair. "Lizzie. I hate that we're fighting."

I look up. *Well, you know how to put an end to it,* I say with my expression.

She pretends not to, but I know she hears me loud and clear. "I'm just not used to it," she continues. "We never fight. I save all that special type of energy for Trish." She gets up and brings the mug to me. "It makes me feel off…unsettled. Could we perhaps—"

"Mom." I stop her. "Can we do this some other time?"

Her face fills with concern. "You're awfully pale. Do you feel okay? I know Willa's home with strep."

And how do you know that? Oh, right, you're dating my former best friend's dad, who is still married to her mom. "I'm fine," I say curtly. "I just have some stuff I have to figure out."

"Anything I can help with?"

I chew on my lip for a second, tempted to tell her all about Trish and the havoc she's wreaked on my life. But something stops me. I'm not sure what. Maybe it's because I know if I do, there's no going back. Any chance for some sort of relationship between me and Trish, however tenuous, would be irreparably damaged. But then again, why should I care? Or even feel that it's important? Is there some law that says sisters have to be friends? *We should, though—shouldn't we?*

"No," I say.

"Okay. If you change your mind, I'm here." She leaves, quietly closing the door behind her.

I skip supper; I'm not hungry. Taco night's coming up soon, but I don't expect to be invited. I crawl into bed, phone clutched in my hand, and pull the covers up over my head. Paranoid that my phone's not working, or that maybe I didn't hear it and missed a text from Willa, I tap the screen with my thumb. It lights up immediately. It's working fine. I scroll through my messages. There's been no text from Willa for ages. I want to tell her that I figured out the baskets and that I'm going to make everything okay. But I am so scared that she won't text back. I keep it on our last conversation thread, tapping the screen every few minutes, just in case, until I fall asleep.

CHAPTER 29

THE NEXT MORNING I DRAG MYSELF DOWN TO THE kitchen, dreading the thought of going to school. I know Mom already left for work. I pray Trish is gone too.

No such luck. She's sitting at the table, chewing on a bagel and working on the word jumble in the newspaper, like it's any other ordinary day.

We don't acknowledge each other.

I pour myself a glass of apple juice. I'm about to down it so I can get out of here when Trish, without looking up, shoves a Tupperware container across the table.

"These are for *you*," she says, all bitchy.

Hey! Might wanna watch your attitude! I grab the container. A note is taped on the top that says, "Lizzie's—no raisins."

I flip the lid off. There's a half dozen homemade muffins inside.

She drops her pencil and looks up. "You know something? I'm not crazy about raisins either."

Just like yesterday, my body stiffens, sensing another battle.

"You have no idea what it's like living with you, do you?" she asks.

"Please, Trish," I say, fake cheery. "Enlighten me."

"Always Mom's perfect little angel. So brilliant. So sweet and kind. I swear she thinks you're a gift from above or something."

What planet is she on? "That's *not* true!"

"No kidding. I'm just as smart as you are. I got early acceptance to Mount A, with a pretty much guaranteed scholarship, but it's like Mom didn't even notice."

"What are you talking about? We went to The Keg for dinner. What did you want? A parade?"

She sticks her nose in the air and doesn't answer.

That is absolutely it. I've had enough. I grab a muffin and start wrapping it in a paper towel.

"You know something else?" she says.

I ignore her and keep wrapping my muffin.

"I've asked to go on the March break Europe trip every year," she continues. "Mom never encouraged *me* to try any fundraising. Didn't even entertain the thought. Not like she did with you. 'Sure honey, can't hurt to give it a shot. If anyone can do it, you can.'" She mimics Mom—badly.

I look at her like she's crazy. "Mom *never* said that! Plus she probably knew you wouldn't stick with any kind of fundraising. That's why she never suggested it! Not to mention, she's not paying for me. I came up with a way to get there myself. You could have too if you'd ever made an effort!"

Her left eye starts to twitch. She's looking sort of scary.

"And how do you think I felt," she says deathly quiet. "About you and Mom and your secret Greg club?"

"*Greg club*? Ha! Trust me. I never wanted to be a member of—wait. Why are you calling it a secret club? You said Mom told you."

"No I didn't. All I said was that I found out. Though I could see how you would think that. I mean, once *you* knew, of course it only makes sense that she would tell me too." She twists up her mouth. "But no. She didn't."

I frown. "Then how did—"

"I overheard you guys fighting."

Something dawns on me. "You were lying, then. You *knew* Willa didn't know about Mom and Greg. You told her on purpose!"

She gives me a smug smile.

"You bitch!" I storm out of the kitchen, feeling the muffin squish in my fist. Scooping up my jacket from the hall bench, I slam the front door behind me as hard as I can.

The wintry air cools my flushed face. Once I'm out of sight of my house, I lean against the nearest tree to try to get my head together. I see my school bus rumble past, down the street to the bus stop. I inch my way around to the far side of the tree so the bus driver doesn't see me. I know he'd be nice and wait.

After the bus pulls away I walk to school. I take my time. I don't care that I'll be late. That's the least of my worries. Trish's words fly around and get all jammed up inside my brain. I can't even think straight. So I try to approach it like a homework assignment—put it in order and address one point at a time.

"I did not *steal* Garret from her," I say out loud. But there's a catch in my voice, just like when I denied it to Trish's face. It *is* true that I didn't steal him, I didn't go chasing after him or anything, but maybe deep down I knew I probably shouldn't have let anything happen between us. The fact that I'd had a crush on him for years, and now he had chosen me…well, I guess I let myself ignore the fact that it never did feel quite right.

She had a point when she said I knew how much she liked him. It was easy to let myself believe she was fine. I wanted so badly for it to be true; that way there'd be no guilt.

It starts to snow. I stop and pull my hat and mitts from my knapsack. Every move I make is a huge exertion on my body. My limbs feel like dead weight. I jam my hat on, tuck in my bangs. *Does Mom really treat me differently than Trish?* She has to, doesn't she? We're two totally different people. I'm sure Mom would have made her raisin-less muffins too, if only she'd asked. And *had* Trish ever said anything about Europe? I don't remember. Maybe.

And as far as the secret club thing goes—it's not like it was on purpose. It didn't really have anything to do with her. Plus, after what she did to Willa, I'm *glad* she felt left out.

First block is almost half over by the time I make it to school. I debate whether or not to slip into class. I might as well. A "late" is better than an "absent." I tell Mr. Mahoney that I missed the bus and had to walk—true-ish.

The rest of my classes go by in a foggy haze. At the end of the day, I come upon Garret at his locker. I back up, turn, and walk in the opposite direction before he notices me, then I duck into the art room. While I hide out, I slump against the door.

A heaviness pushes down on my chest. I roll over and inch one eyeball to the edge of the glass panel that runs along the side of the door. The hall is empty except for Mr. Scott, who's talking to Constable Miller, our school's liaison officer. My head starts to swim and my vision blurs a little. *What are they talking about? He was really serious about bringing in the police.* I roll back against the door and wait until the room stops spinning. It takes a while.

I gotta do something.

So I do.

At the main office, I stop at the reception counter. "Is Mr. Scott here?" I ask the secretary.

She nods, shuffling through a stack of paper.

"Do you think I could see him?"

"Name?" she asks glancing up at me over the rim of her glasses.

"Lizzie Turner."

She presses a button on her phone. "Mr. Scott. There's a Lizzie Turner here to see you."

"Send her in," a voice crackles back over the intercom.

"Go ahead," she says.

"Thanks."

Mr. Scott's door is open. He's sitting behind his desk, looking exactly as he did a few days ago, with what seems like the same pile of folders spread out in front of him. Makes me wonder if he ever left.

He gestures to a chair on the other side of his desk. "Have a seat."

I draw a shaky breath and sit.

"What can I do for you?"

"I, um…the other day…well, I lied. And so I came to confess…well, partly confess."

His eyebrows knit together. "Please. Continue."

"It was me," I say. "I'm The Goodbye Girls. Or girl," I correct. "I needed money to go on the New York trip, so I came up with this idea to break up with people for a fee." I let all the words tumble out of me before I change my mind.

Mr. Scott steeples his fingers and leans back in his chair. "I confess, Lizzie. I'm very disappointed. I wouldn't have expected this from you. But like I mentioned, I've been wrong before…."

"I did *not* do those other baskets. The mean ones." I say it firmly because it's the truth. "I had nothing to do with them." I can live with taking responsibility for the stuff I *did* do. There's no way I'm taking responsibility for the stuff I didn't.

He stays quiet for a minute. "What about your friend, Ms. Carlson?"

I shake my head. "She didn't have anything to do with it. She has tonnes of money." I keep shaking my head. "Nope. No need to do anything like this."

"I see." He stays quiet for a minute, just looking at me, like he's trying to figure something out. "This operation must have been quite the undertaking."

"Yup." I hope my face isn't as red as it feels.

"I remember taking down your posters. Though a part of me appreciates your entrepreneurial spirit, I have to question the moral implications."

I stare down at my hands folded on my lap.

"I mean, profiting from other people's misery," he clarifies.

I want to say, "They were all going to break up anyway," but I don't.

"And I'm sure there must be something in our policy about using school property to perpetuate a business of this sort, as in one for your own personal gain," he continues.

I want to argue this point too. Because we didn't use school property. But again I keep my mouth shut and stay focused on my hands.

He doesn't say anything for so long, I look up. He's tapping his still-steepled fingers against his lips. If he's trying to make me sweat, it's working.

"Now that you've confessed to being the one behind these Goodbye Girls, Lizzie, why should I believe that you are responsible for only some baskets and not others?"

I can see where he's coming from. I mean, why confess at all in the first place? I'm not even sure what I'd hoped to accomplish—maybe just to make it all stop. After thinking hard, trying to come up with some sort of answer, I rip a page from Trish's book and use almost her exact words. "Do you actually believe I would send a basket like that to my *own* sister? That's pretty harsh."

"I suppose you have a point. Though I've been a high school principal for over ten years. Nothing really surprises me anymore."

I give him a weak smile.

"As you well know, Trisha was very upset by this whole thing."

"Yes. It was devastating," I say, trying to sound sincere.

"What I still can't understand is, why would someone target your sister, Allan, and Olivia, and then name you as the mastermind behind it all?"

I don't answer.

"Are you sure that it just didn't go off the rails somewhere?" he presses. "Maybe you got talked or pressured into doing a few things that maybe you're not proud of? You know, if that's the case, now's the time to come clean."

"I'm telling you the truth, Mr. Scott. I *did* do the original breakup baskets, but I promise you, I didn't do those last three."

He keeps looking at me, as if he's waiting for me to crack or something. Then he says, "And you can't think of anyone—an enemy, perhaps—who *would* have?"

A mental image of the photo I took of Bradley's email forms clearly in my mind. My phone is in my pocket, only inches from my hand. My thumb twitches, like it's itching to pull the trigger. A million thoughts race through my head. *Do I give Trish up? Why should I take the bullet for her? She would never do it for me. The choice is clear, isn't it? I have a school record to protect too. But if I do give her up, what does that say about me? That I'm a vindictive bitch like her? And if she misses her chance at a scholarship, do I really want her here, with me, for the next who knows how many years? She would be unbearable to live with. Maybe I'm more selfish than I think I am….*

With my heart smacking against my ribs, I lower my eyes, and say, "I have no idea."

I hope he hasn't taken a course on reading body language, although it probably should be mandatory for high school principals.

He clears his throat loudly. "I'll be honest. I don't have much to work with here. No one has made a complaint other than your sister, but she didn't give me anything to go on. I very much believe the police should be involved, but I will need her to come back in and tell them her story, make a statement."

I jerk my head up. "Wait. You mean you'll only get the police involved if Trish wants you to?"

"Well, yes. But if no one *wants* to get the police involved…." He shrugs. "There's not much I can do. I can't force them. Thus far, there're no leads, no proof."

I let his words sink in. "I don't think she wants to pursue it," I say slowly.

His forehead creases in a frown. "I find that hard to believe. She must want to know who did this to her. She is the only one who's come in to talk to me. She knows how serious this is. I'm still hoping she can convince Allan and Olivia to come in as well."

"Actually, I think she's pretty much over it now." I swallow down a huge wad of something stuck in my throat. "She told me all she wanted to do is to put it behind her and move on. You know, focus on her last semester of high school."

He gives me a doubtful look.

"So am I in trouble, sir?" I ask, hoping to distract him from all my lies. "Like, for The Goodbye Girls stuff?"

Not answering right away, he opens a file folder. I assume it's mine. His eyes travel down the page. "I see your name is on the list for the New York trip, so your business venture obviously paid off," he says, a tinge of disapproval in his voice.

He's going to ban me from the trip. Then all of a sudden it hits me. *Do it.* I don't even want to go anymore. Why would I? Willa and I have been dreaming about it forever, but now we're not even speaking. If I go on the trip, all I'll get is icy silence. I'm not close to anyone else in band. There's Garret, but I can't glom onto him the entire time. I know my fantasy New York romance can't really come true on a band trip. I'll end up sharing a room with some random girls. It's not a dream, it's a nightmare.

"I'm not going on the trip," I say.

His eyes widen.

"Yeah." I nod my head. "I'm not going on the trip," I say it a little louder this time.

"May I ask why?" he says quietly.

Feeling my eyes start to sting, I blink a few times. "Personal reasons."

"I hope nothing serious."

"No, no." I have to keep blinking so the water doesn't come out. "Just something came up." I jump up from my chair. "Can I go? I forgot my mom's picking me up," I lie.

"Of course." He politely stands. "But could you please encourage your sister to change her mind and come back in? Tomorrow's the last day before Christmas break, but if she comes to see me in the morning, I can arrange a meeting with Constable Miller in the afternoon, if that's the direction she chooses."

"Yeah, sure," I say as I practically run from his office, down the hall, and into the girls' bathroom. Once I check under all the stalls and know for sure that I'm alone, I hang over the sink and let the tears come.

CHAPTER 30

THE NEXT DAY GOES BY PAINFULLY SLOWLY. THE school's clocks *must* be broken. It takes forever for the bells to ring. Doesn't matter much. Hardly anyone showed up for classes, deciding to get a head start on their Christmas vacation. *But not me. Good ol' Lizzie never misses a class.*

I gather my things from my locker. When I slam the door it echoes through the empty hall. Even the nerdy keeners make it out before me. The last few whiz by, trying to make the bus. Guess they have lives too. Everyone but me. I slowly shuffle my way down to the front entrance. All the classroom doors are flung wide open, most of the chairs already stacked on the desks, ready for one last cleaning. No staff or teachers staying late today.

As I round the corner, I hear a loud ticking coming from the band room. Mr. Fraser is sitting on a stool with headphones on, tapping his baton against a metal music stand. I hesitate outside his door. I was going to send him an email, but he's here now, so I might as well finish ripping off the Band-Aid.

"Mr. Fraser?" I edge closer and repeat his name a couple times till he finally hears me.

"Oh, hey, Lizzie." He smiles, takes off his headphones, and lets them hang around his neck. "I was just listening to that symphony from our last class. You guys are sounding pretty good."

I force myself to smile back. "That's great."

"What can I do for you?" He snaps his finger. "You're probably here to make your last payment."

"No, no. It's not that. I, uh…actually, Mr. Fraser, I've decided not to go on the trip."

He frowns and sits down behind his desk. "But Lizzie, why?"

"It's, um, personal reasons."

"Is there anything I can do?"

"No, it's—no, nothing. Thank you, though."

He opens a drawer and takes out a black notebook. "I'm sorry to lose you, Lizzie. You're a strong flute player, the band's going to miss you."

"Thank you," I whisper.

"Are you sure you won't change your mind?"

"Yes, I'm sure."

He leans back in his chair and flips open the notebook. "Unfortunately, because you're cancelling so late, you won't get your deposit back."

"I know."

"But I can write you a cheque for the rest of what you've paid." He does some scribbling and then rips the cheque from the book.

"Thanks." I fold it up and slip it into my back pocket without even looking at it.

"And again. I'm sorry you won't be joining us. I hope everything works out."

I feel myself starting to blink again. The tears are on their way back. I force another smile and leave before I collapse into a soggy puddle on the floor.

It's almost dark when the school doors finally swing closed behind me. I walk down the path that runs between the school and the library. My phone chirps. It's Garret.

Still haven't seen u. U ok?

Ya sorry, I lie. I had tons of work to finish before break.

Where u now?

Leaving school on path to lib, I text. Though it takes me a while. In spite of the cold, my fingers are sweaty and slip on the screen.

Gr8 I'm at cgc I'll come meet u we can go home together.

I get a sick feeling in my stomach. I start to text, I'm not sure we should see each—then I gasp. Jesus. I hold down the backspace. I was about to break up with Garret via text just like Todd did to Abby. I shake my head. That text was the seed from which the whole idea for The Goodbye Girls grew.

I text, Ok.

The Canada Games Centre is right across the street from the library. Garret is crossing the parking lot by the time I emerge from the wooded path. He waves and jogs toward me. He smiles his perfect smile with his super white teeth. It almost takes my breath away. But then the sick feeling in my stomach returns with a vengeance. It's all I can do not to double over.

"Hey, stranger," he says.

"Hey," I say.

"I was beginning to think you were avoiding me."

I don't answer. I just give him my best fake laugh.

"So to kick off vacay, a bunch of us are going skating at the Oval tonight. Wanna come?"

"I don't have skates," I say quickly.

"That's okay. They have ones there to borrow. For free."

"Garret…" My heart starts thumping. I take a deep breath in through my nose, out through my mouth. "You're one of the nicest guys I've ever met, but I don't think we should see each other anymore."

His head jerks back. "Really?"

"It's all my fault. It's nothing you've done or anything."

"Your fault." He frowns, thinking for a minute. "Is this about Trish?"

I nod. "Sort of. She said she was fine with me seeing you. But she wasn't. And I should have known she wasn't."

He thinks some more. "I guess I always knew that might be a problem."

"No. It's on me."

"Did she say something to you?"

I swallow and lie. "No, I can just tell."

"I see her and Jordan hanging out together a lot. She always looks happy."

"Yeah." I shrug. "Looks can be deceiving."

"It's too bad," he says. "I like you."

"I like you too."

"And I can't change your mind?"

"No."

We stand there awkwardly, not knowing what to say.

He looks over his shoulder. "The bus is coming. Should we grab it?"

"No." I shake my head. "You go. I was heading for the library anyway. I have some books on hold."

"Oh, okay." His cheeks turn red. "Guess I won't see you till the trip then, so…uh…Merry Christmas."

"Yeah, same to you," I say softly, staring down at my feet. I can't risk letting him see my face.

I wait in the library vestibule, blinking back tears, watching as Garret gets on the bus and the doors close behind him. When it pulls away into traffic, I leave the library and slowly walk home.

Some time later, I find myself in the kitchen—I must have been on autopilot.

Mom is at the sink draining pasta into a colander. She takes one look at me and says, "Lizzie, what happened?"

I just stand there.

She pulls out a kitchen chair. "Sit down and tell me what's wrong."

I don't sit down, I kick the chair instead. "You wanna know what's wrong? I'll tell you what's wrong. You're going out with Willa's dad. You wouldn't let me tell her. She found out. And then she found out I knew. And now she's not talking to me. JUST LIKE I SAID WOULD HAPPEN. My sister's a bitch. I just broke up with a guy I really like. And, oh yeah. I'm not going on the trip to New York."

"Willa knows?" Mom lowers herself onto a kitchen chair. "She hasn't said a word to Greg."

"Gee, thanks, Mom!" I shout. "Thanks for focusing on *that* instead of the fact that I'm not going on the trip!"

Her face drains of colour. "Oh my god, Lizzie." She holds her hands to her cheeks. "You're absolutely right. I'm *so* sorry."

I shake my head. "Save it."

"No, seriously." She reaches an arm toward me. "Tell me why. I thought you raised all your money. If you need more, let me help. I'll get a cash advance on the credit card."

"No, Mom. It's too late."

"I mean it. I'll make up the difference. You were so excited. I want you to go."

"No, Mom," I repeat. "That won't fix anything!" For some reason, the more she offers to help, the more angry it makes me.

"Is this about Willa, then?" She wrings her hands. "I should have suspected something. I haven't seen her around in a couple days."

"*A couple days*, Mom?! Try over a *week!*"

She lets out a little gasp and mouths, "Over a week?" like she can't believe it, then, "I think you should know, Lizzie, Willa told her mom she didn't want to go on the trip."

I digest this information, but don't say anything.

"Marlene had to pass that development onto Greg, because Willa refuses to see or speak to him. He assumes it's because they signed the divorce papers last week—"

"They did?" *Willa's worst nightmare.*

"Marlene's making Willa go, though. Says she's been in such a funk, she thinks it will do her good."

I continue to digest the information, letting it roll around in my head. Is Willa's funk because of the divorce? Greg and Mom? Or me? Whatever it is, the funk can't be that debilitating if she's still heading to New York. "Yeah, well, she couldn't have put up *that* much of a fight. Since when does she let Marlene tell her what to do?" I say sarcastically.

"Lizzie, please. Could we just take a moment and talk about this reasonably?"

I stare back at her. Not really at her, more like past her. There's a faint ringing in my ears. Could be the exhaustion.

"You know what? I'm done talking." What little bit of energy I have left kicks in. "You, Greg, Willa, Trish! You guys can figure this all out yourselves! Willa can go to New York! Trish can destroy the human race! You and Greg can run away to Vegas for all I care! You have my blessing!" By the time I finish, I'm waving my arms around like one of those inflatable arm-flailing guys you see in front of car dealerships.

"Lizzie, sit—"

"Mom! No. I said I'm done." If I'd been holding a mic, I would have dropped it for dramatic effect.

"You can't expect me to just leave things like this. You're breaking my heart. Can't we please talk about this?"

My eyes get wide. *Oh my god. If she says "talk" one more time….*

The car dealership inflatable guy has lost all his air. I got nothin' left. "Mom," I whisper, "I've told you what's going on. Please let that be enough for now."

She studies me for a minute, biting her lip. "Okay."

I go out to the hall and drop my coat on the bench. She follows me. "What can I do to make you feel better? Do you want some supper? I'll make you anything you want."

"I don't want anything."

"Well, what are you doing now?"

"Bed." I reach for the banister. "I'm going to bed."

CHAPTER 31

TRISH OPENS MY BEDROOM DOOR WITHOUT KNOCK-ing. *Shit. I forgot to relock it after the bathroom.* There have been numerous knob rattlings and knocks since yesterday. I ignored them all.

"You might as well go ahead and tell me," she says, folding her arms.

I look up from my laptop. My new passion is solitaire. I've been playing pretty much non-stop for the last day and a half, and I'm not thrilled about being interrupted. "Tell you what?"

"Did you talk to Mr. Scott?"

I lower my eyes and click away at a few keys.

"Lizzie. Did you?"

"It's Christmas vacation," I say. "How could I talk to Mr. Scott?"

"Before school ended," she says. "Did you talk to him before school ended?"

I keep playing my game. I like seeing her squirm. The way things are going for me right now, I have to take my joy when I can get it.

"Look," she huffs. "Just tell me if I have to spend the entire break waiting for the cops to show up on the doorstep."

I toy with the idea of letting her dangle in the wind for the next week or so, but truthfully I just want her out of my room and I know she won't let it go until I answer.

"You're *fine*," I say. "Don't worry about it."

"Oh." She continues to stand there. "But did you talk to him?"

"Trish." I slam my laptop closed. "I said don't worry about it. What more do you want?"

"Okay. Jesus!" She starts to close my door, then stops. "No. Wait. Tell me what happened."

"No." *Why should I?*

"I'm not leaving till you do."

"Fine!" I say through my teeth. "I told him I was the one behind The Goodbye Girls, but that I didn't do those other baskets, and I had no idea who did."

"And that was it? He was okay with that?"

"Yup."

She squints at me. "What about the police?"

"He doesn't have any proof of anything, and no one's even made a complaint except you. So the police will only get involved if you *want* them to get involved." I give her a nasty smirk. "Figured you didn't want that."

The relief is obvious on her face. "And you didn't get in trouble?"

"What do you care?" I reopen my laptop. "Shut the door on your way out."

She hesitates again for a moment but then leaves, shutting the door behind her.

A new hand of solitaire hasn't even finished dealing itself on my screen when there's a knock.

"*What?*" I call.

Trish sticks her head in. "I just got this tote bag. It's brand new. See?" She holds it up. "Tags still on. I thought it might be good on the plane. It'll fit your laptop."

"I'm not going on the trip," I say, glancing up from the screen.

Trish's mouth falls open. "What? Why?"

"I'm just *not*. And it's none of your business."

"But…" She tugs on her lip. "Did Mr. Scott kick you off?"

"I *said*, it's none of your business."

"Well…is it to do with Willa, then? Is *she* still going?"

"What do you think?" I snap.

Looking confused, Trish backs out of my doorway. Once I hear it click shut, I go onto The Goodbye Girls's website. I don't even know why; I haven't looked at it in a couple weeks. The screen reads, "This page is no longer available." My eyes drift to my dresser, to my sock drawer in particular. I get up, yank it open, and reach in the back for the envelope. I flick through the bills, counting under my breath, then mentally add on the refund cheque that I haven't cashed yet. Half this money is Willa's. I think about walking to the bank and depositing all of it so I can send her an e-transfer. She could spend the money in New York. Then I change my mind. She probably has lots of spending money.

Usually I live for Christmas break. But not this time. This time I barely leave my room, or my bed for that matter. Why would I? What reason could I possibly have? Mom keeps trying to lure me out using Christmas cookies and fudge, as if I'm some wounded animal hiding in the bush.

"It's Christmas Eve, Lizzie," Mom says. "Why don't you get out of bed and come carolling with the Sampsons? Their kids adore you."

I want to say I'd rather stick a fork in my eyeball, but instead I fake croak, "I've got a sore throat."

"At least come with us and drink hot chocolate. You don't have to sing."

"I can't. I can't even swallow."

She looks at me like she knows I'm lying. But she says, "All right," and comes back with a glass of water and a couple Advil anyway.

Later, I recognize sounds from downstairs. The tinkling of bells. I know Mom and Trish are watching *It's a Wonderful Life*. We watch it every Christmas Eve. I jam in my headphones to drown it out.

I finally come out Christmas morning for our gift exchange. It's a quiet, solemn affair. Thank god we bought gifts while we were all still talking to each other.

Mom makes the exact same breakfast as she does every Christmas morning—fruit salad, Belgian waffles, bacon, hash browns, and cinnamon buns. She puts everything on the table with a huge smile plastered on her face, probably hoping it's contagious.

We start eating. The clinking of the utensils sound extra loud against the lack of conversation.

"Come on, ladies," Mom says, all chipper. "It's Christmas. Whatever it is you two are fighting about"—she looks at me—"and whatever our issues are, let's put it aside for today."

Trish and I just keep chewing.

Mom sighs loudly and adds about a half a bottle of Baileys to her coffee.

"It's almost time to go to Mrs. Mitchell's," Mom says, standing at the end of my bed. "You should get up and get dressed."

Ever since Dad died, the Mitchells have had us for Christmas dinner. Mrs. Mitchell's intentions are good, but she makes literally the worst turkey in the history of the world. It's so dry, it's like gnawing on straw. We've tried a couple of times to get out of it, make up some excuse, but she won't hear of it, and changes her schedule to fit ours. We're in too deep. There's no getting out.

"I'm not going," I say. "I have a migraine."

"Lizzie. It would do—"

"Mom, please."

Trish comes up behind her. "What's goin' on?"

"Your sister's not feeling well," Mom says. "Again."

Trish looks at me, then says, "That's okay, Mom. Let her stay home. More turkey shoe leather for us."

After they leave, I get up and go to my dresser in search of a clean T-shirt. I've had the same one on for a few days now. I'm starting to offend even myself. When I open the top drawer I see a plastic bag and pull it out. It's my Christmas present for Willa. I got her a really nice leather passport cover with a matching luggage tag and change purse. I should have just given it to her. Too late now. Might as well return it. I can't use it. I'm not going anywhere.

I stuff it all back in the drawer, crawl into bed, and pull the duvet over my head.

I must have fallen asleep because the next thing I see is Mom leaning over me with her hand pressed against my forehead. "You don't have a fever. How are you feeling?"

"Okay."

"Well, I managed to talk Mrs. Mitchell out of sending you a turkey dinner to go, but she wouldn't let me leave without a slab of fruitcake. She says the rum will help your headache."

"Gross."

"I think I threw my back out carrying it home. I swear it weighs twenty pounds."

"Gross," I repeat, and pull the duvet back up over my head.

One day of vacation blurs into the next. Except for the odd shower, I haven't been out of my Roots sweatpants in eight days. Before I know it, it's New Year's Eve. Trish is going to some party; even Mom has plans. Probably with Greg. She tells me she's going to cancel them because she doesn't want me to be alone. Why can't she get it through her head that that's exactly what I want? So I lie and say I'm going to Becca's to watch the ball drop. I don't even know a Becca. It just pops into my head because she was my favourite Bachelorette.

When I'm sure the house is empty, I tiptoe downstairs. My legs actually creak and groan due to lack of use. I curl up on the sofa and eat an entire family size bag of Doritos while I watch Ryan Seacrest's *New Year's Rockin' Eve*—just in case there's a quiz later. I'm back in bed pretending to be asleep when I hear Trish, and then Mom, come home.

I drag my laptop onto my stomach and open it up to my most recent game of solitaire. *Will this vacation ever end?* I don't know how much longer I can do this. But then I cringe because the alternative is school. I glance down at the time and date on the bottom of the screen. My stomach takes a little dip. They leave today for New York. Everybody will be heading to the airport in a few hours. Tonight they'll have dinner at the hotel and then off to *Phantom*. Tomorrow most of the day will be spent at the Met. People say you can spend days in there. My lower lip starts to tremble and I bite it to make it stop. It doesn't work. My lip keeps trembling. Then from nowhere, these noisy, snotty sobs burst from my body, accompanied with a non-stop raging river of tears. I curl up into the fetal position and let it all out till there's nothing left.

My eyes still feel swollen and puffy from my long night of crying. There are a dozen balled-up Kleenexes scattered all over my bed, and a dozen more on the floor around my garbage can where I threw and missed. I don't bother to pick any up and roll back into the fetal position. I'm facing my open laptop. The Facebook icon glows bright blue on my tool bar, taunting me. I refuse to give in and click on it. I know it's just going to be a barrage of pics and comments from everyone who's in New York. About all their adventures. I reach over and delete the bookmark. "That takes care of that," I say.

Eventually I roll over the other way. Trish is standing in my doorway, her phone in her hand. "Um, Abby just texted me...."

I prop myself up on one elbow and try to focus on Trish, who is much farther away than my eyes have looked in days. "Yeah?"

"She's on the trip. With Garret."

"Yeah? So?" I have zero patience.

She frowns. "She says Garret asked Maddy Evans to the prom. Did it right on the front steps of the Met in front of everyone."

My heart beats a few extra beats. "Good for him." I try to sound like I don't care.

Trish is still frowning. "But I thought—"

"You thought *what*, Trish?" *Can't everyone just leave me alone?*

She opens her mouth, but closes it again. Then she leans against the door frame. "He's not all perfect, you know."

"Oh?"

"Yeah. He's a real heavy mouth breather."

I raise my eyebrows.

"At first you don't think it's going to be a big deal, but after a while…."

I just shake my head, burrow down, and hide under my duvet.

I attempt to put drops in my eyes—they're dry and irritated from gazing into the computer screen for days on end. Or maybe from my epic crying session. I'm dabbing my face with a Kleenex when there's a knock on my door. I rest my head back against the headboard. *God. Let me play my solitaire in peace!* "Yes?!" I shout.

"It's me, honey," Mom says.

"Yes?" I repeat.

She comes over and sits on the edge of my bed. "So, listen. There's an advertising rep who's a client at the gym. She works at Q104. You know, the radio station?"

I have to stop myself from sighing. "Yes, Mom. I know what Q104 is."

She waves a hand in the air. "Of course you do. Anyhow… she gave me a couple passes to an advance screening of that new Leonardo DiCaprio movie. You know how we love our Leo."

She's right. We do love our Leo.

It might even be worth getting out of bed for. I'm about to ask her when it is, when I pause. Something occurs to me. "You know, Mom," I say, "I know someone else who likes Leo."

"Oh. Who?"

"Trish." *At least I assume she does, because, like, who doesn't?*

"Really?"

"Yeah. She does."

Mom shrugs. "Well, here." She sets the passes down beside me. "You and Trish go, then."

"No, no." I slide them back toward her. "*You* and Trish go."

She tilts her head. "It's highly unlikely Trish will want to go to a movie with me, her mother."

"Actually, Mom, I think it's *highly* likely."

My phone chirps, startling me awake from my now routine sucky-vacation evening nap. I haven't gotten a text in forever. The phone's buried in my bed somewhere and it takes me a moment to find it. There, up in the corner. A message from Willa. Worried I'm hallucinating, I rub my eyes and check again before opening it.

Heard u and garret broke up.

Yup.

U ok?

Then it happens. That cement block that has been sitting on my chest slowly starts crumbling to dust, and I can finally breathe normally again.

Yup I'm ok.

Talk when I get back.

Sure.

I lie there for a minute, letting it sink in. I can't be sure, but I think I feel the corners of my mouth turn up, just a bit, all by themselves.

The opening theme of *Jeopardy* drifts up from the living room TV. I flip myself out of bed, tug off my sweats and T-shirt, and slip on jeans and my West hoodie.

At the top of the stairs I lean over the rail. Mom and Trish are sitting together on the couch frantically shouting out wrong questions for the answer. As I make my way down to join them, I holler, "Whoever doesn't get Final Jeopardy has to eat Mrs. Mitchell's fruitcake!"

ACKNOWLEDGEMENTS

So many people to thank.

First, my family. Ross, for your constant support. Lexi and William, for providing an endless supply of material, letting me use you as a sounding board, and for shooting down my ideas when you knew they wouldn't work. My puppy, Hermione, for keeping my feet warm as I typed every word.

Thank you to my editor, Penelope Jackson. I felt like you "got me." Not everyone does.

To Whitney Moran, and the whole team at Nimbus. Thank you for making the experience seamless and easy.

Lastly, my writing group. Jo Ann Yhard, Daphne Greer, Graham Bullock, Jennifer Thorne, Joanna Butler, and Lexi Harrington. Your amazing talent is reflected in every page.

(An honorary shout-out to Taylor Swift, whose text-message breakup inspired the idea for this story.)

WILLIAM HARRINGTON

L ISA HARRINGTON'S NOVELS INCLUDE *Twisted*, shortlisted for the Canadian Library Association's YA Book of the year, *Live to Tell*, winner of the White Pine, Ann Connor Brimer, and SYRCA Snow Willow Awards, and *Rattled*, published in 2010 to critical praise. Her work has also appeared in *A Maritime Christmas*. Lisa lives in Halifax with her family and puppy, Hermione. Visit Lisa online at lisaharrington.ca